EGRESS / ˈiːgrɛs, ...

1 the act of leaving a place; emergence.

2 the way of leaving; an opening or exit.

EGRESS

NEW OPENINGS IN LITERARY ART

EDITORS

David Winters

Andrew Latimer

ILLUSTRATION

Catrin Morgan

DESIGN

Andrew Latimer

Jessica Kelly

PUBLISHED BY

Little Island Press

SUBSCRIPTION

£12 per issue ; £20 per annum

INFO (ISSN 2515-2491)

ISBN 978-1-9998549-2-8

CONTACT

egress@littleislandpress.co.uk

twitter.com/EgressMag

www.littleislandpress.co.uk/egress

HOW REVOLUTIONS BEGIN.

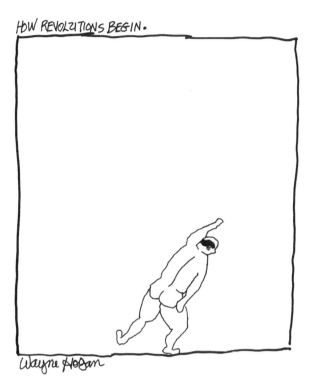

Wayne Hogan

Nicole Treska

A Hole Burned through the Middle of Everything

We stalled again, and then we died. It was hot inside, and even though the windows were down, the wind wasn't blowing our way. I strained to find first and engage the clutch. I let it pop up and pressed the gas, but too fast; the engine caught for a moment, in bright hope, then choked and we were going nowhere – beached and blue in the middle of the intersection, under a sky just as blue, but moving. Amber sat shotgun, foot out the window, resting on the side-view. Pigeons swooped overhead in lazy ovals – silver when they circled near, black dots when they winged away; then near again, then away, then gone.

'It's about listening,' Amber said. She tapped at her ear and pushed the mirror around with her big toe, so it searched the street behind us in sharp, short close-ups. She was teaching me to drive stick because she was blind and drunk and couldn't.

'Just listen. The engine will tell you. You'll figure it out. You'll have to.'

We were both tired from drinking late into the night before. Drunk, the thought of Amber teaching me to drive was a plan as good as any. The finer points wore wineskates and looped elaborate figure-of-eights through our future, which we admired, gliding toward blackout.

Now – in the morning, in the truck, in the traffic – now we were in deep.

'I think it might be about more than listening,' I yelled across the long bench. The engine stalled again and again and my hangover burned across the back of my skull. My right arm was sore from turning the key, which had imprinted itself on my thumb. With my left arm I did big windmills out the window, imploring people to go around, *just go around*. But the light changed from green to yellow to red, and no one moved. It was quiet in the intersection until the cross-walk started its heavy click. Amber turned fast toward the sound. Her smile spread out from the center and faded at the edges.

'See? See?' She held one wavering finger up, like her point held the answer I needed, like I could start the car with what she was about to say. 'Just listen! See? I told you. Didn't I tell you? You don't even need to see.'

She whistled a short burst of notes and looked in my direction, squinting one eye to hold me whole. 'Do you know what song that is?'

She was still drunk; she was drunk anew. I heard her whistling, but I couldn't answer. Her eyes were a riot. And the cars spilling over the hill behind us? The gazes in the rearview were a riot, too. And the wind through the silver leaves of the birch trees? A riot. And my heart. My heart beating in my chest was a riot.

I wanted horns, or sirens, or a sharp impact to rip me up and fling me elsewhere, anywhere elsewhere. Weeds the emerald color of fancier plants sprung up hip-high on the sidewalks. Next to me, Amber's gaze had gone somewhere private.

In the night we drank red wine until the rain put us inside and '*incurable*' and '*accelerated*' became abstractions in the fuzzy-dark of the little house. We drank until we laughed about it.

'*You* fell down the stairs, and *I'm* the blind one?'

Or, 'God grant me the serenity to accept the things I cannot see.'

Or, 'What doesn't kill you makes you blinder.'

Before I passed out, bloody kneed and upright, I promised I'd drive her truck home.

In the morning, the wind had picked up. I watched the clouds skitter and poured my third coffee. Amber switched to a real drink – filled a mason jar with ice, gin, grapefruit juice, a tall stick of rosemary. 'Muscle memory,' she said, wiping the counter with a paper towel.

'Looks like today's the big day,' she said. 'Learn something new, like I say, or die trying.' She stirred her herb stick, smiled into her drink. Then she came and sat right up next to me, spilling her gin over her lap, and stage-whispered, 'I don't really know what today looks like.' Her chuckle was hoarse from cigarettes and booze, and her free hand mimed violent explosions. 'There's a hole burned through the middle of everything.'

The retina records what you see and sends the image to your brain. When the macula – a tiny oval in the retina – deteriorates, you lose acuity from the inside out. You lose the fine detail. Then all the detail. Then you lose everything.

I turned the key and stamped the pedals in the right order, by miraculous accident. It wasn't elegant, but I'll tell you this: sometimes there is no quick enough escape from where you are.

I found second, straight south. Amber smiled into the new breeze of our movement and said, 'You pick shit up pretty quick when you have to. Maybe things aren't so bad, after all.' She closed her eyes, turned her face side to side to feel it all over. She brought the jar of clear stuff from her purse to her lips in a smooth motion, then used her arm to wipe her mouth, shoulder straight down to elbow. 'Shift!' She shouted.

She was listening for the whine, for that sustained *vvvvvvv* of impatience that signaled something overdue. When she heard it, high and urgent, she said, 'Ok, good. Up to third, and easy. I need this truck, now more than ever.'

I shifted to third, but I couldn't tell between roar and rev. Strange thing to say, *now more than ever*. But what did I know about what she needed? And how do you help someone lose everything?

. . .

Amber used to sell diamonds on cruise ships. Used to hold the tiny specks of fire and move her hand to catch the light until the rocks exploded with brilliance. She was an expert at catching the shine – a top salesgirl. The trick, she said, was not to let on that you were playing with people's perception. She could spot a mark the second they stepped in, see the want all over their faces.

After that, we waited tables, and Amber caught the shine there, too. Night after night she made big eyes at the big money guys and coaxed them to order from the bottom of the list – down where the triple-digit wines were, and the big commissions. We drank their leftovers and made good money. We fucked the line cooks and the club members, after work, in the sand, against the sea wall. We were so young.

During split-shifts, we'd swim. The water was deep and clear, and eels and reef sharks hunted below. We never wore our jewelry in the water. Sharks don't eat humans, but in the blur of the ocean, flashes of silver and gold can trick the eye. Even a shark's eye, which can see through blur.

'They have a blind spot on their snout,' Amber would say, as we started through the channel, her stroke sure and constant. 'So, if you're lucky enough to see it coming, go for the snout.'

She never wore goggles. She said she'd rather not see it coming.

· · ·

Once the truck got going, the engine moved under its own turning and I rested my hand loose on the knob. The trees that lined the road sang with bird noise and foliage. Amber was looking out the car window. She could see the sky, but not the clouds thinning into atmosphere.

'I haven't stopped drinking since I saw the doctor,' she said. I didn't ask how long. 'Everything is unreal. Faces started disappearing on me, like a nightmare. One day I see you, the next day you're gone. And you know what's wild? I don't even miss them that much – the faces. People are easier out of focus.'

The road rolled on uninterrupted ahead of us for a long while, and the wind rushed through the cab, puffing our shirts out against our seatbelts in that summer way. Our hair flailed and whipped and the tires lapped a lopsided rhythm. We passed a sign announcing the onramp, and I read it out loud. For a while everything was fine – we talked about the past, because the past was easier to map than the future.

'Can you see my face?' I asked, taking my eyes off the road to look at her. It seemed important that she see me.

'Watch the road. One of us should.'

She opened her phone and read a text from her ex, from whom we'd taken big Baby Blue. She held the screen up to her nose to see the words.

'He can't believe I took it. He thinks he gets to keep my *anything*? If I can't keep anything, he can't either. You hear that? He gets nothing of me. Shift into fourth, now, Jesus, can't you hear?'

The clutch was heavy, and I held it down hard with my toes. I leaned forward on the big bench seat and jammed the gearshift down to the right – snug into fourth. The gears were so loose the shift nearly kissed the floorboards on its way down. The truck idled a beat, then caught, then went faster. The sun made sharp lines across soft lawns as it moved toward the top of the sky. Amber let her fingers swim through the airstream out the window, and said she should have known.

'I saw it with my own eyes,' she said.

We passed block after block of houses with swing sets and open screen doors, and all of it was so golden and nice in the morning, it burst my heart to look.

Gary Lutz

Am I Keeping You?

They gave my mother seven months. After that, the ground was just one more thing over her head.

It's a wonder I can remember my father for anything other than running off with a woman who did not so much come into the picture as black everything else out. But I was young, eleven, twelve, with plenty of time for time, and I didn't mind that everything had been left up to my aunts. They were all on my mother's side, these overwiped women of long silences and ruckled smileage, and they one by one took me in to take me apart.

The first aunt had a monitoring eye and fed me from flatware that looked too wide for any mouth. There was a lot of fabric under her roof, cottons and linens — balloon cloth, clokay, huckaback, georgette, express stripe, whipcord. But I never once saw a sewing machine or even so much as a needle and thread. She told me to get out of the house and bounce a ball. 'You meet people that way,' she said. I did meet a girl, older, with a batch of acne and darkened, doused-looking eyes and dimmed hair that one minute was stilled with clips and pins and the next minute seemed to be sinking back into her skull. She grabbed my ball, tossed the thing into a tree, then exempted herself from her dress, an airy rayonesquerie of a thing, balled it up, took me all around her body to where it was open and raw, and that's where I saw the thing that stuck out, a thing that could not have just come out of nowhere. She warned me that her heart had long been laid to rest in somebody else, a sister, and this was a sister whose breasts were precise little integers and whose fingers, dunked into mackinaw pockets, were tipped with nails snipped to the quick but painted, whole-coloredly, the daylight-blue of however much was left of a day you had to decide whether to get broken up that very instant in whichever way you saw fit or else honor the cracks you'd already been finding within it – so what exactly did I propose to offer? Her knees gleamed futilely. A hand of hers was already escorting one of my mine along her cheek, her throat, then lower and lower down. Then her hand hardened boldly onto the bones of my own. I must have decided not to stick around to see how the rest of any strings might get pulled.

The next aunt lived with an eliminated middleman. He had once sold storm windows. I might as well still picture him as a man forever driving at what he should have long ago walked away from. The few things he had done had always lacked a certain doneness. There was always something missing from the finish. This aunt let the days flake away and of course had her reasons. 'Don't keep looking to me for everything,' she'd say. 'Look out a window.' And, sure enough, in any such light, it helped to know whether it was blood or just chocolate you were suddenly spitting out.

This aunt could never see herself outshining a child, but there she was with two daughters, neither one a marrier. They were, the both of them, overgrown, unconformed to each other, activatedly morbid, denied even a stylish and successful loneliness. They came from either end of the same generation and had dodged their lives as best they could. The sticking point was that each had her own room in that deep, wide-winding house. The first one kept repeating, *If something were to happen to me* as if it were the most hopeful thing in this world a person could get said. I had to cup my ears to hear her. She was the tiptoeing sort. She was pretty-spoken but had pageants of pain in her face. Her dress was one of those filmier things that looked as if it had just breezed over her from nowhere mappable in this hemisphere. She had a shoulder bag packed with backward-read paperbacks pampered with wax-papered covers. There were two electric fans in her room, three speeds each, and she knew which settings in which combination would be needed to muffle whatever she was up to, if only turning pages.

She got me alone in the bathroom one night when I really had to go. 'We're not to flush,' she said. 'Pee in the sink. That's how the other men do it. It's called consideration.' I did as I was told, and she said that the joke was on the older kids in some really close family, a giddily tight-knit one, because what could they do but get even closer and then grow up and have to marry outside of it anyway? It was just one of many thoughts of hers that turned thoughtless in my mocking turnings of them. But it turned out we were both afraid of the exact same two things: rats and travel.

I think she actually did think our hearts would one day come brawling toward each other in a full and tiring life. And I did reach for her ropingly that once. I must have kissed her, I guess, and I must have grubbed around in my mind for somebody more puppety to think about. I must have settled for a small-mouthed tablemate from school, a kid whose blunted brainage had put him on the map. (The kid was always in the news. His inner world was said to be full of outspread spaces. Things would slide out of his hands because they didn't want to stay there. When he opened his mouth, parts of speech dropped out.)

Her kisses, though, came back measuringly. What they were measuring was anyone's guess. She would go to her grave sexually unscathed.

As for her sister, she was grown up or at least was finished with becoming something. She worked at a courtesy counter and picked all day long at something incipiently sicklied on her arm. She had a dank voice, and a youthless drift to her eyes, and there was hardly any swank to her hair, which was long but not of its time. She survived from one interim to the next in those strappy open shoes that offered brute displays of her every haggard toe. The kinds of baths she took left her looking even blearier. She lived in fear of the hot-water heater – that it could blow at any moment. So she kept her things, anything of import, propped atop plastic crates. 'But you live upstairs,' I assured her. 'Hot water rises,' she said. I never expected to see her arms swinging that martially. I wondered when the chair in the sitting room had become *her* chair. She sat in it because it faced away from the window. The window gave out on the garage, but the car was kept out front. In a vase was a splurge of plucked and skinkled thistles, and in her brassiere she climbed over hulky furniture to a stepladder that led her to where she hoarded words for some forthcoming bedpost ballad of the obvious. I got to know her fingerwise and by mouth but never nailed her motive.

If my history is correct, this was a house in which one room led directly into another and then another without the relief, the solace, of halls, hallways. I should not have to spell it out that for the longest time – months, no doubt – I had been wanted on the phone. I would set aside whatever I was up to (by now I had picked up a skill or two) and make my way to the room where the receiver awaited me. The phone was on a part of the floor I never knew my way well enough around. A tangle of cords pulled me down into what I want to think of as a swimmer's stance, the crawl of somebody athletic in water.

I was expected to talk. I answered in a voice that sounded as if it were sealing itself off from within.

It was another aunt calling. 'Drop whatever you're doing,' she said.

I kept my grip on that barbellish old phone. The talking was all up to her.

'If you're even doing anything, right? Because what would a son of my sister's have to do? I assume you've been hearing it night and day about your mother? And your father – you're in on it? Or you're just bashful? You've been fazed? You're nobody's sunshine now?'

It was thus I was handed off to this next aunt. She never brought up my parents again, but on a shelf was a photograph of them at a frankfurter shack on a play-park boardwalk. I looked at the two of them flaunting life and limb in sun-lotioned leisure. I was expected to live and learn right then and there? The photograph was in a side room with curtains that curtained off only certain parts of things, watershed bric-a-brac never to be touched. My aunt motioned me to a seat on the sofa. Was she pulling my leg when she said she had wanted children because she assumed they would come with answers, or because she wanted somebody to look after her when she was dead? I did not ask about any of them. I did not even know how many of them there might have been, or how long ago they had filed out of the family. She was in her fifties now, she said, and the pills did not go down right. It was always the longest day of the year, she said. No matter how fiercely she felt the hours grouped and grouping around her, she liked to talk about the people who ailed her, but she had a squelchy way of telling people off. I must have yawned, or done something too fussingly with my hands, for she got up and showed me to what would have to do for my room. The only other beings in the house were low to the ground and stole in at night to draw off the little they could of my warmth. I gather that I no longer scorched.

I often got towed off further than needed in my sleep.

A leg of hers, crepe-papery, twined around one of mine, other fleshes of hers cresting against my side – I'd awaken in the aunt's widespread bed to her air-bursts, her intakes, and I would pore over her to the point of despoilery.

Then one day a son of hers who was said to have left no trace was suddenly, distantly, back. (Hadn't someone once told me that the homely always return home?) This son had the upstairs and left an awful lot up to the eye of the beholder. That body of his was far too big a thing on him, for starters, and the life asurge in it surged obscurely. I had to get used to him, though. Things happened, in fact, inside of a week. He liked to come out from behind a night's showing of beard to get blunt again about our places and duties on the bed.

'We're not roommates,' he insisted. 'We live in the same room. There is a difference.'

We shared the towel, though, damp as it always was, and all those sticky salads he threw together, salads he militarized with smeared meats and spottled chocolate.

The safety goggles never came off as he ate.

The drinks he slurked out of a measuring cup were at bottom mostly cludded sugar.

He was forlorn because there was nothing to look forward to in pornography anymore. In the snaggily handwritten notes he wrote to me at night, he added bonus letters to the spelling of almost every other word. The notes concerned his having pressed down on the accelerator of his car only to hear the middle C of a giant, plucked string. But the car, he'd decided, was not speaking on his behalf.

He led me in what he said would be half an hour of exercise – the stretches and lifts, the slaps and shrivels. A couple of unorganized birthmarks on the left side of his neck gave it that dirtied look. The hair on his legs was as unflourishing as a girl's.

He inquired about my hiding-places, any milestones put off, welcomes worn out, my rights and dislikes, anything I had yet to take a slam at.

I remember whole mouthfuls of what I told him. It came out uncomely spoken, and lacking in exact words.

But by then, his mother had caught an interesting cold, one that could advance in any number of directions, so would any of us care to venture a guess as to what would be first to redden?

The eyes, I figured? Those scringing, scummed-up, stinkpot eyes?

Then one morning I felt all motory, like things were about to get going. I involved a whole arm of his in the one thing I didn't care to keep doing to myself. There must have been more and more of a bodily situation of this sort over the weeks, because, you are sure to remember, girls were cutting corners and going directly to other girls anyway. Because, to repeat, any woman with a man is only a woman with a man.

Everybody knows this, but they forget to build their lives around it.

Even worse: no carpeting beneath us, just a green baize, and then, to get out, there was one of those doors destitute of knob or handle: you had to plump yourself against it to get the thing open.

That city, if you could call it that, was just soiled scenery against which people kept letting the moment pass. I walked unfollowed to the bus shelter and waited. I let the first bus go by, then a second. I turned them all down. It was an afternoon of wasteful wavings-away. Then an aunt showed up showily in a taxi. For once, there was too much sun. She had her hand planed out visorwise or as a salute.

This fourth aunt was the youngest. Don't look here for a list of her failings, her college troubles, her wrongs and belongings. Don't look here for any settled description of the rougher stuff in her diet. I can't really order her all the way back into the order of things. She liked to drop friends and pose problems in public. Nobody had ever taught her how to feel left out. She liked to loiter where the action was, even when her luck was running late. But having a kid, she said, had felt like getting fucked from the inside out. She inflicted the whole battery of motherly emotion onto the kid, and halfway through toddlerhood, the path the kid's legs took and the path the kid's arms took didn't always overlap even notionally. The kid had trouble keeping weight on her, problems with holding a shape. The kid grew up to have an indoor disposition and learned that, when there were people around, it was just enough to help them on again with their coats and then get them going. Would I ever meet this girl?, I wondered, but my aunt made fun of me for even asking. She said she wanted me to leave her as I'd found her – a woman I'd otherwise one day be in a position to insert some rocks inside. The line-up of her fingers on my arm that afternoon left a permanent burn.

But the day came when I was old enough to live on my own, old enough to wonder what I should want of myself, just how far I could count on myself, and then I discovered women close to my age and then the women's unabsorbed men and then the women again with the men no longer much to care about. I tended to avoid people who were larger than life, but one of them had rigged things so that the only life any larger than hers was her own. You never could tell how close to sit or how far out she might spiral.

It was a midland city we were in, a city beset by seagulls.

The city was built just far enough up to ensure a tight squeeze among the people fleeing.

Outgoing buses had all been painted to look like trolley cars.

Stamps that year featured the faces of intemperate-looking inventors, and there were new bounces to any life sidelined from its better nature.

Written up in the municipal literature was a restaurant where the dining parties were led into little closets to sit. You were welcome to eat as long and as alone as you liked. You could let the meal mudge itself around inside of you. You could come close to your life yet not be taken in. It was expected that you would think back on people who had trailed away from you in average time or to whom you had never quite come right out and said, 'Don't do this to me.' The line always stretched around the block.

Everywhere you looked, people had been portioned into apartments in which there was always some creakage from above, and somebody always allowed you to stay long enough to hear her say, 'Do you have any idea what that fucking person is doing up there? That fucking person is about to put on a pair of pants.'

It's a touchy subject, I know, but the thing about living in cities is that somebody was already doing something exactly as you would have done it, so you were excused.

Plus, you could thin out your things with walks to corner trash baskets. You could make one offering to each. One after another of the houseplants you'd slain. Lumps of soap dulled of any sandalwood. Old school papers, with that immemorial finish to those widths of arithmetic.

Eventually you'd have to work, of course, but there was certain to be a woman at work whose bosom looked lugged in obvious, gutsy suffering. In fact, she'd spoken to you exactly once. 'The thing is this,' she'd begun.

I worked, you see, for some weather service. I was a receptionist first, then a secretary. Clerkly, low-salaried, overridden in everything, I wore workwear sewn roomily and was admirably undistracted.

I deposited the for-deposit-only checks in person at a bank with a limestone front. The teller there was a man around my age who wrote things on the back of each receipt – pleasantries, predictions. I would turn them over as I gained the street: 'Have a good evening. You will come to discover that selfhood is not a victimless crime.'

I lived on my own that year and loved the cubing efficiency of my room. I would sit hot-stomached in a dark that felt adhesive. I would let the nights get plastered to me. I'd crawl to the fridge and say, 'Let's see, let me see.' In my sleep, if it came, I was good at pulling things out by their roots.

Work and apartment – I had just those two stations in life, wearing out the one through the other and improving on neither. But the streets between them were busy with people getting zeals out of their systems. People rovingly lonesome with brains apatter and nobody to stamp anything out. The woman who gave me that packetful of smidges of hair scritched from her legs, her underarms. The blinkful lady who claimed that the actual set of her features misrepresented her beyond all libel. That girl with the stormish eyes and strayaway incisors, who grilled me gently about birth-order lore, then deepened my vocabulary with 'banishee,' 'platonic parent.' Should I have felt nothing but a deadweight sympathy anyway?

All I know is that late one afternoon I felt pulled into a museum, a low-vaulted hall of art, and the things dearest to me in there were the pedestals, the prop-ups, the bases. The actual statuarial crap, the sculptures and suchnot, were a little too humany for me in the mood I couldn't see myself losing soon. Afterward, though, I sat thoughtfully in a stall in the restroom off the lobby and listened to the pips and petite ruptions of my neighbor. Then he was suddenly, mouthily, vocal through the partition, though he rapped on it a few times first. 'I'm only here for the day,' the neighbor said. 'Can you beat that? Have you ever been here for only one day? Or are you here every day? Round the clock? Watchman? That must be it. I can sense things about you, guardianly things, just from the way you hold your quiet. Can you tell me something? What is it you can tell me of everything? Can you help me lose even a little of my life?'

I waited until he lost faith and, unflushing, emerged. Then I heard the squiss of the faucet, the roaring of the hand-dryer, the ungracious progress of feet toward the door.[1]

---

[1] The man had left a note, though, on the sink – a sheet of paper folded in half, and with many a puncture where the pencil had poked through: 'Those so inclined to have ever gazed hopefully into the waters with a mind to undertaking a taxonomy of discharge, whether or not the

In sum: you grow up, you grow a little too much in one year, you pass for a toothpick in another, you look to your fingers only to see what they are just now letting go of – I can give you only an estimate of what I must have felt for any of the people who mobilized themselves so hurtedly. There was always something I'd know before I knew it. Even, I mean, if all there was to know was that from any window in the world the world itself always looked awfully sure of itself?

So mustn't we thus come, at last, to my one unbettered wife?

I was forty-four; she had barely been dipped coldly out of her twenties when we met, though this was her third marriage. Word was she'd been thrown from the first. Nobody could have been sold on the second. One day, she claimed, it just felt adjourned. The husband's love gave out, or something. She walked away from the house, made it as far as the corner, and there

---

specimens have been left to stand for only minutes, or, less happily, been allowed for a good hour or more to drift or disperse or spoil or mature (and let us assume, of course, that the produce has not been obscured by a gauzy haze of tissue) – those souls, I wager, would count themselves among the first to admit to an unsatisfying recourse to the classificatory terminologies of other sciences, whether it be the dreamy nomenclature of cloud figurations or the crisper formulations of the geomorphologist; and to compound the disappointment, once in a great while there appears a comprehensive evacuation, a single but multiphase release, that embraces

I was, on a side street, looking a tree up and down. It was a cloud-laden morning, and I was unculminated.

It may be well to explain that in what became our house, several avenues over, I covered the doorknobs and other household projections with taped paper warnings out of fear that, astoop for this or that dropped earstopper, I'd crack a tooth or put out an eye. I had to know what to watch out for.

And she, this dangerously natured woman of unshimmering wealth, didn't believe in utensils, or openers. If something had to come in a can, you were probably not meant to have it.

May I have more of a say about this union? My wife and I were the wrong people, yes, but the same general type. A love of a kind might be said to have been caused to happen, but any new day was just a mongrel of everything a day ago. Must I go into the pinprick nicks of time we lived in? We wrote to each other on noteboards. 'Later', one of us would venture. Or:

---

a full range of phenomena – first, a barely discernible basal formation of firm, introductory issue settled deep in the throat of the bowl (countable units, say, appearing as constellatory pellets or, less often, as broken sausageal curlings); and, second, above and around this foundation, a stewy diarrheal guck, or slatter; and finally, centered at the top, and the first to meet the eye, a thick, compacted puddlelike and perfectly circular floating mass (the 'mudpie', as children sometimes are apt to put it) – and such a one, vented to confound and defeat even the most determined of catalogists among us, you will here have found.'

'Until very soon.' But in actual moments of domestic civility, she would budge the evening forward toward dinnertime, bathtime, bedtime. When you made everything just a *time,* please understand, duration was less of a niggling, streaming thing, and more of a bearable stagger. I answered her phone in a voice smokily close to her own, held entire incensed chitchats that way with her parents and brother. Any sex I had with her was less and less collaborative, rarely frontal or topical, barely even in person. Besides, she had backup loves, a specified fruitsomeness to her breath, a maiden name no one dared undo. In no time, there were country-wide, gutted schools of thought about us in widening, spurning circles of friends washing their hands first of her, then of me, and what's there to keep me from saying, even this late, that I would rather there had been facts of life different from the ones there actually were? But I knew her in the absolute.

So: per my ex-wife per the woman she next favored (though nothing in the world seemed to have much of anything left of her impress) per the girl next in line for her (this one, as well, had never been one to dwell all that easily in twos and threes) per some later soundsick intimate of my own (his kisses were spitty and pushy and must have gone right through me to whomever he was after) per a narrow-hearted party in whose lopsided eyes there was neither hokum nor hoopla (but who soon preferred muddling herself away on some other party) per the lately unpeeped-at person now collectedly typing these words:

Life gets old.

It stunts your growth.

This was by now in the day and age of my early sixties.

I was a gala wreckage of decades, I guess.

I had a hash of thinning hair. I always ate out for a lesser chance of choking alone.

At work, the emphasis had long since shifted to forecasts for tri-state areas, then later for city-states. There was money in what I did, yes, but then, all of a sudden, people no longer wanted it done, or I no longer could do it. Either way, the money went all wrong.

And there were no longer any people in my life to speak of, though one day the daughter of the youngest aunt showed up with the news that all of the aunts were dead. Their final sayings had all been taken down, if I was interested.

She wanted ice water in a pitcher. She liked the bouncy-ball sound the old refrigerator made when I closed the door.

She'd had a couple of kids too late, she said, and they weren't the sturdy little stalks of childhood she'd been led to expect but just scoops of flesh, mucks of skin and vein, and she'd left them with her husband and left him for an unsunned sliver of a woman who liked to be around people when they were whispering about the unending finishing-off of a friendship, liking it even better when it was up to her to see to it that another of them got steered beyond the brink.

These were brazenly globuled tears to behold.

So could I put her up?

Her name now was a strange choice of words, her hair was a mown brown, and she insisted her arms smelled differently – the left one like cinnamon, the right one like burnt cloves.

She needed to get things off her chest, she said. One I remember: Never keep anything on the passenger seat of your car. Not even a flashlight or a map. People will know how often nobody else ever sits beside you there.

And another: Never expect more of a greeting than *You again*.

She was soon speaking of the few people she'd been you-know-who to.

I let her talk, because anything you could put into words could be taken right back out, and who was I not to concede that people like her (this included me) knew our place – it's just that we were determined never to set foot there? This explained all the extra, oppositive steps that had to be figured into everything.

Plus she wanted to know whether our doctors even knew we were alive.

She stayed a few days, she needed to sleep with a nosebleed hankie under her pillow just in case, and when she slept, even the plainest of the day's emotions were left strewn on her face. She found a job where sickly wheels of tomato had to be lowered onto the bigger wheels of the meat. Then, one morning, there was the newly razored gooseflesh of her legs, and things must have gotten a little too one-on-one. I recited the thing about how I had all the time in her world but who knows how much left in mine. She was quick to agree grievously to how easy it was to fit everything so snugly into a duffle. Then the bare arm trending toward me, looking exercised but unendeavoring. Then just the minutes until the cab finally came.

From a dredger of dusting powder she left behind, I applied some of the baby-pink to my cheek. How soon until it could turn to soot to suit me?

She went back to her husband, I later learned. They had a place built out in Parkwood, Woodside, Sidegate – one of those.

People will go ahead and tell you that the rest of it all happened punctually – the mandatory 'phased retirement,' as they now called it in Human Resources. Half the hours, half the pay, but full health.

That was the year, mind you, when keys were cut with too long a stem. They kept breaking off in the locks. It was forever hell to get yourself back inside. Worse, the world had sorted itself out into the people you once might have been and the people you never now would be. The only other person left who still had a key to my place was somebody recent at work, a level-chested, emotionally unassembled woman with deep-set, practically impacted eyes. Teeth stacked anew, paprika-colored hair looking capped on. Not one mole on the narrow barrel of her throat. She was tight-mouthed but spoke several long-quieted languages, sometimes in homemade words of her own.

From the oyster-white ovality of her face, she told of days that stalked her all their length. She chased after sleep and looked to her dreams for entertainment, but the dreams sputtered away before she could play enough of a part in how things turned out. Her sleep was rarely to her liking. She bought the popular book that advised thinking of the bed as the vehicle, not the destination. 'Treat the bed with care,' the book said in the woofery voice that came out of me whenever I now read aloud. 'Have it inspected. Dress it sensibly.' We had a stopgap set of bedclothes made out of old ponchos and peignoirs. But still she struggled. For a while, I kept my life catercorner to hers. In concerted secrecy, we observed disturbances of wedlock through oriel windows. We unnamed a neighbor's dog. Mornings, we would back off from ourselves in verdictive light that the blinds shredded onto the floor.

Then one day there was a gargly, submarine quality to her voice. The words came out funny. She talked paltrily of 'travelling pains'.

The earliest the specialist could see her was in five days, but she stopped thinking 'days' and instead 'sets of hours,' which could be as long or as short as she wished them to be, so she made five hours equal a set, which pushed the appointment a full twenty-four sets of hours safely away.

But every day covered her with new colorations.

The doctor called it a rot caught too late.

On my account, she made sure her final steps in retreat were loud and countable.

I let an hour or two pass for things to sink in before I set out to search for her on the fundamental avenue, in the arterial complicacy of the central streets, along the slants and crookings of residential lanes.

I could see everything through the weather but her.

I came back, jumbled through her stuff. Spilled sortings of skirt buttons, jiggly piles of underapparel, a pillow yet to be dandled – I wasn't a handyman. I had no handyman solutions to any of it.

The signature of her lips left on a glass – such are things best left unwashed.

In her purse: the spring and silvery push-button and further internals of what was once a ballpoint pen; dimmed dimes; an outfolded candy-bar wrapper on whose glossy inner surface were handwritten figures that had been taken up in rash multiplication with an eyebrow pencil (projected earnings, payouts?).

I fell asleep on the dolled-up bed until the new day's sky was already incurring its surety of blue.

The first few days streamed out of the week and into a memory of minutes here and there of not yet being unpaired. Then a sign that had always said 'IN-DOOR POOL' got itself painted over.

A counselor ventured that the mistake might have been in picturing the matrimonious state as a territory, a body of land, then treating it *geographically* – having both parties agree on how farther off each of us should have looked to each other when seen even further from afar.

'We weren't married,' I told him.

I was referred to another counselor, who counselled me that people don't change, but the ways you look for them do.

'You'll hear eventually,' he said.

Meaning, I took it, that in years to come, the worst that could've been asked of me if I did not answer the door right away was 'Do you have anyone else with you in there?'

Further, you can fend off your body for only so long. You sooner or later have to have your look at it, even if just in the long view. There needn't be a scrutiny. Besides, it was like me to have always taken my baths in the dark. One night in the tub, though, I felt something of myself, caught a touch of something more than what had once belonged there.

The thing was the size of a golf ball when I went for the first ultrasound. The woman in the clowny scrubs was young, mid-twenties, at most. Everything about her seemed untapered, untucked. But why the decanters, the candlestands, the candles burned almost all the way down? This was a clinic, a lab at a medical park.

She wielded the wand with a distaste I must have craved. Her voice now and then released a meager dirge. I was in there for twenty, twenty-five minutes.

A doctor called the next day with results. He sounded elderly, pronounced the diagnosis (*hydrocele* : an inwash and pooling of something liquidy into the tissue or whatnot protecting a testicle, if I heard him right), and said they had found quite a bit of debris in there, too.

I naturally did nothing for months. Why worry about a little water or whatever this fluid amounted to down in that pouch when I now had my whole life behind me to drain?

The thing was as big as a tennis ball when I went in for a second test.

The technician this time was older, maybe fifty, with that detailed allure of someone having long welcomed a life of edifying carnal blight. She was bold of hand. The procedure felt more like a massage – lots of brushy sweeps of the upper leg with one hand, the other hand guiding the wand. I could sense her talent relaxing itself. She made me feel endorsed.

'Touched less as a kid than later?' she asked at some point.

'Not much really either time.'

Then, from her: 'Might I be critical of you? Look, I've known you – *of* you – for half an hour, hardly.'

'Please do.'

'Your body is making a scene. But in my line of work, these are a dime a dozen. What are your plans?'

I said nothing.

'It will get bigger,' she said. 'It'll keep filling up in there. Don't think it won't. I've seen these things get bigger than a grapefruit.'

Still nothing from me.

'What use are you getting out of any of it anyway?'

I went back to my place, divided the bedroom into quadrants, fractionary zones (each with a theme, a motif), though a lot of good that would ever do.

This was not a lively disease, no question, and not even a disease at all, and less a condition than a predicament, a flooded scrotal circumstance, but also no question was that I kept getting baggier and baggier down there by the week.

Months more. Called the doctor again. Said the doctor: 'Come in, my friend, and I do mean friend. A buddy of mine'll numb you, we'll get out the syphons, it'll be over and done within minutes, you'll walk out of here lighter on your feet. And it's just a co-pay, pal. That sound good, my young man?'

But, knowing me, knowing myself, I went out to find a cutter. Not the kind the kids had become. I mean the other kind. But the only one in town was doing only abortions now. 'Tell you what,' she said over the phone. 'Come on over anyways.'

This was in an apartment tower revised into a condo block. Nothing leathern or left-behind-looking in the lobby. I took the elevator up, found her unit, knocked. She opened the door in just a general way. I was in the vague myself.

Inside, beneath a high-arched ceiling, I found her to be clear-faced, upright in tunic and tights, hair provoked into roils of sorrel. (Her ring finger had a surplus ring.)

'Why don't we just see it and go from there?' she said.

She busied herself believably with one of the reins of her necklace.

I disrobed my lower half.

'So we'll just throw the babies out with the bath-water?' she said, surveying. 'That what you have in mind?'

I was all nods.

She shut her eyes and spoke to me in some stab at a parable about the kind of men who had ever made it this far.

This sounded like a Bible-study lesson. My face must have gone wavy.

'Okay, so let's not be so imaginative then,' she said. 'Let's not think things too far through. Let's just take simple things simply. This might just be the simplest thing.'

While she talked, she no longer seemed to be stirring other, unspoken words inside her, and when she went quiet for a little, I figured she wasn't thinking hard at all.

'Something the size of a tennis ball might need nothing more than a tennis racquet taken to it, agreed?' she said. 'We won't even have to get medical or anything.'

And it so happened she had a racquet, she said, recently restrung. It was just a matter of fetching it from a far-off room, farther off than a visitor might first have envisioned. (That vaulted place of hers must have been practically arcaded. There were roundels, too.) While she was gone (a quarter-hour?), I eventually found the chapel where towels were kept and laid some out.

Back, she said, 'Okay? You won't be a baby?'

Then started whacking.

A few sovereign bashes, then the things just dropped off.

The blood might have been lush, but there wasn't even all that much of it.

'See, mostly like water anyway,' she said. 'No mystique. Didn't I tell you?'

Then sutures stitched with a sprung safety pin instead of any needle.

'You'll feel it for a few. No big decisions for a couple days.'

I reached for my underslacks, my slacks, then my wallet in the slacks.

She said my money was no good in that part of her life.

I dressed, rode the elevator down, hailed a taxi.

I called off a week's worth of work. I took a leave to give my groin leisure to spoil and swell. I let it redden debonairly. I skipped the dressings, the ice packs, the tablets to degrade the pain. I sent no infection away.

Within months, with nothing much of its own to do, my dick had dwindled a little, and this too was a boon.

I was pegged ever after as the person who sat way at the back of the last planetarium left in that neck of the woods and stared at whatever stars the operator would get slung up. I liked feeling covered by a fake, finite sky, and I liked how shifty a night sky was supposed to make you feel. I don't think the guy ever even knew he had an audience until I would clear my throat, or crackle a chocolate-bar wrapper, and he would dial the house lights up all the way in retribution. There was a rail built into the back of the row of seats in front of me, and I must have always been gripping the thing pretty possessively when I always said, 'Do you take requests?'

This fellow, of course, ignored me.

Outside, afterward, the world would look planetary not at all. Everything looked overpainted. There was a glister over all of it. There were just close-going roads and streets, low-set buildings, people, not many, and there was nothing – not one thing – that said the most or even the least about me. I could not see even any of the people looking my way.

But answer me this: by how many minutes, how many days – or months, years, however you want to figure it – must you keep insisting that life is too short?

I'm not keeping you, am I?

Am I keeping you?

Is that what it is?

Then what else is it, then?

Mother!

What else can the dead be taught?

Victoria Lancelotta

Accident, Design

In the house that is barely a house Roy kisses June's skin, the smooth dips and raised puckerings, the lilac scars and the furred petals. He kisses all of it. Outside the ground is wet and the sky is lead and inside he runs his hands over ruins and fortune.

The house stands on blocks that are sinking. Its windows are insulated with heavy plastic and the roof with tarpaper. The rooms, front and kitchen and bed, smell of oil soap, apples and tea. June does not wear perfume. She wears long skirts, wool socks and heavy boots, sweaters whose sleeves reach to her fingertips, wound scarves. She wears a different face every day. Roy loves all of them.

She is lucky and its opposite: she has been opened up and rearranged, fixed as far as fixing goes, closed up with pricking stitches. On the way home from a party she'd unlatched her seatbelt to reach for a fallen glove and when the car flipped that was enough for her to sail through the exploded window, to land on iced and broken ground while in what was left of the back seat, clothing fused to bubbling skin. She is new but not improved and what does this matter anyway, what difference to Roy, she is exactly as she has been since she knocked on his door and asked if he could call a cab to take her back to town.

Town is far but home was farther.

I'm sorry to bother you, she said that night, but sometimes I get confused. Do you have a phone?

I don't think it was my fault, she said the morning after that night – the crash, I mean – but sometimes I'm not sure.

Roy has been patient, he is patient. It is his nature. He does not know hers, yet.

• • •

Roy's mother pulls her hair up into a high ponytail, tight enough to smooth her forehead, lift her brows. Eyeliner and mascara but no lipstick, perfume sprayed on her throat, wrists, inside the waistband of her jeans. Hoop earrings, the gold flaking off at the closures. More eyeliner, more mascara.

Lipstick smears off anyway: onto cigarettes, glasses, skin.

The trick is knowing which tricks to know.

She packs her purse with a makeup bag, lighter and cigarettes, sunglasses even though it's November and dark already by five o'clock, a tin of Vaseline, peppermint candy.

Eight ball, nine ball, one-pocket. She'll have a cigarette and then leave for the bus stop to catch the number three and be in the smoky warmth of the Last Resort by seven-thirty, Wheel of Fortune muted on the TV above the bar, Boston or Foghat on the jukebox, spiced rum and Sprite with lime in front of her. The last time she saw her son was when she'd slipped onto a stool beside a wide back in a coat she didn't know. She'd swiveled and laid a hand on that blind and promising expanse of wool then frozen when he turned to face her. The coat, the beard, the cap pulled low – a mistake anyone could make. She tried to speak and he recoiled as though she were licking flames.

• • •

Town is six blocks of dollar stores and convenience marts, buffets and drive-thrus, then miles of narrow roads that snake out toward ravines and woods, toward flat-roofed houses set low on shallow lots, a rocky creek behind them and the steep reach of hills behind that, trees bare and damp.

To find Roy's mother on a Friday: go to the Last Resort on the corner of East and Valley, to the short bar next to the pool table.

On a Wednesday: go to the VFW hall, to the card room in the back.

On a Thursday: go to the truck stop at exit 26.

• • •

Roy dropped out of school at fourteen and no one noticed. He baled hay and handled stock, assembled media consoles on one factory floor, tanned leather on another. He opened an account at a bank across town, kept his deposit slips in an envelope in a box of laundry detergent on his closet shelf. He learned to drive and learned to sew and learned to become invisible in the house he shared with his mother and the men who came and stayed a night or a week or a year, the men who looked at him with contempt if he was lucky and loathing if he was not. He learned to fight back.

He reads the newspaper, he reads the farm report, he reads the turned-out leaves in the saucer of his teacup. He knows that he cannot entirely rely on the information he derives from any of these sources and he knows he has no choice.

He knows the first chapters of *Treasure Island* and *The Old Man and the Sea* by heart, and *The Rime of the Ancient Mariner*. He knows when to cover the garden rows with soft pine in winter and how to sedate the blind dog to pull a broken tooth. He knows every road that spokes from town: the crumbling asphalt that climbs almost to the ridgeline, the highway to the interstate and the two-lane's graceful swerve into towns that may or may not be like this one, filled with girls that may or not be like her. Except: he doesn't know any girls like her, he doesn't know her. Her skin tastes of smoke and berries, ash and blood.

He doesn't know if her name is really June. When he asked her that first night she hesitated in telling him, just long enough.

• • •

His mother zips her jacket against the wind at the bus stop and Roy spreads June open in the wide bed. Between them, the town breathes under shadows and sky, between mud and mountains. In the spring the sun finds side ways in through its long setting, between new green leaves, between carports and fences. In November it fades falling before dinners have been set out. The trees are naked and shaking, too weak to hold it up.

Roy's mother waits in the street light's sodium glow, eating peanut butter cheese crackers from crinkling plastic. Her fingers are bright orange and salty. The bus schedules vary by neighborhood: extended nighttime routes by the college to the north, every fifteen minutes starting at four a.m. in a nine-mile radius of the milk processing plant, a constant eastern curve around the paint factory and the hang of thick pink smoke above it.

She is thirty-eight years old and the wrong kind of thin. Her cheeks and hands are chapped rough and the skin on her forearms and chest is the mottled blue of a waiting bruise but she can remember even so what it was like to look in a mirror and see nothing that needed fixing, or hiding.

Before her son, for example. She was perfect: fourteen years old, a long dark braid and brown shoulders, sundress straps twisted into uneven bows. The boys in homeroom liked to tug that braid and so did Uncle Al, who was not her uncle but her mother's boyfriend, who had a car that filled their driveway with hot metal, who let her sit in the driver's seat and rest her hands on the leather-wrapped wheel that was bigger than the pizzas he bought for the three of them to eat on Saturday nights. Her mother insisted they eat the pizzas with knives and forks, because Uncle Al was from the city – he had city manners and city money and he left behind a pile of it after bending her over her twin bed with the daisy sheets and the ruffled pillowcases, after doing what all the boys in homeroom must've wanted to do, after easing that bright blinding car out of their driveway and steering it back to the city before her mother even woke.

She hears the bus before she sees it, an oily wheeze; crumples the crackers' plastic wrapper and drops it back into her purse.

Those pillowcases with their pink and yellow flowers, Uncle Al's rough cheek against her back, the cedar and musk of his aftershave, his mint-hot breath.

His mother climbs into the blue warmth of the bus and Roy presses his face into the crook of June's elbows, the soft crease of her hips. Her skin feels aqueous against his lips. He has never seen an ocean but her eyes are very blue. Sometimes they lose focus and sometimes they burn straight through him.

• • •

June: a pile of bloody rags by the skid and muddy rut but breathing, ambulance lights cherry swirls in the smoke, in the gasoline sky, in the melting glass. When they peeled her from the punched earth, quartz winked hot from her flesh.

Paramedics, nurses, surgeons, king's horses and men; articulate fingers, too many to count, all of them gloved and slick with blood but dexterous, precise. Accident, then design.

I used to be pretty, she said to Roy the second night, by way of an explanation he hadn't asked for, her voice empty of regret or grief. I have pictures if you want to see them.

He didn't. What do I need pictures for when you're right here? he said, and she coiled herself around him, her hair matted and dull in the lamplight, honeysuckle arms ragged and veined. She didn't ask to stay and he didn't say to leave and the second night multiplied by five, by fifteen. Winter is still weeks away but already it gnaws at the days' brittle edges.

He has in a box a stack of photographs he bought for a dollar at a junk sale: blue-black oceans, jagged icebergs, deserts glowing red. When she goes, which he knows she will, he will still be able to look at what he's never seen.

• • •

At the Last Resort Roy's mother follows a man down the back hallway and out through the fire door while June slips from the bed where Roy lies sleeping. The smooth planked floor is cool under her bare feet but the kitchen is warm, embers still red and snapping in the stove and the blind dog sleeping next to it, curled and breathing on a torn fold of quilt.

She loves the dog, its careful paws and milk-blue eyes, the strawberry nose that is never still. She will miss it.

The man works wrinkled bills from the front pocket of his jeans and Roy's mother shivers, winter at the back of her neck. She knows him by sight but not by name – town is not that small anymore. It has crept, lot by house by mailbox on post, over gully and field; it has clawed up the dirt slopes of the piedmont.

By sight: reddish hair and reddish eyes and sunken in the chest and cheeks, wind burned there. He comes on Fridays nights, mostly alone but sometimes walking slow beside a woman who holds his arm with one hand and the rubber grip of a cane with the other, her drag of bent leg a grappling hook. She doesn't ask where the woman is tonight.

The river twists black. It swallows the careless, but only in spring.

Roy's mother takes the money with the equanimity of someone who believes she's already earned it. June – of course her name is June but she would answer to any month – pours a glass of water and sinks down to the floor. The dog rests its long muzzle on her bare leg, sighs without waking.

Town is full of dogs less lucky. It is full of buck-shot stop signs and trucks with perforated fenders, bitches chained to the metal beds, teats stretched and bitten raw. Town sees nothing and hears less. It turns its stony face away.

Cannula, hound and hyena, cautery and stitch. Roy sleeps. June hasn't decided which face she will keep. In the alley behind the Last Resort twenty dollars might as well be a million.

· · ·

In the morning Roy goes to the river, sinks heel-deep into the sucking mud at the steep edge of it and casts his line. The sky hangs gray, ready to split with rain. He can feel the house behind him, warming his back with June's heavy sleep.

He reels in pike and smallmouth, hooks a finger through each set of gills and pulls it through to break the necks, lays the silver bodies across wet rocks.

Show me, she said, the first time he'd brought a fish from the river and laid it on newspapers on the table, and she watched him scale and slit, work his fingers in to drag the guts free, snip the fins. Her eyes were nickel-bright.

He's turned both ankles on the stony apron of this mountain, gone blue at the lips and fingers in January water, broken wrists against the needled ground. He's taken fish and rabbit, wild garlic, ramps and fiddle-head, mustard flower.

Let me, she said the next time he brought fish from the river, and he did. The knife loved her hands, their sure and bloody grace. She slipped the blade around the gills and under the spine, lifted the bony column free of the long body while he watched.

Ironic, she said, smiling crooked. I mean –

I know what you mean, he said.

Sometimes he imagines walking her naked into the woods, her wrists in his hand at the base of her spine, that sweet dip where he'd kick just hard enough to send her hands-and-knees to the ground, her sugar-white ass and the muddy soles of her feet to the sky.

Pretty is an accident, Roy thinks. Pretty is the opposite of the spindling trees, the gashed slope and river. It is nothing he is interested in. Her face without scars is not hers. It does not belong to him. It does not belong anywhere.

He tucks the fish into his creel and starts back to the house. He would do anything to keep her.

• • •

In the morning Roy's mother covers her hair with a paper cap and punches in for her shift at the hospital cafeteria.

Accidents happen, there are no accidents – she has never been able to decide which she believes.

She believes in destiny, not luck; fate, not chance.

The first time she saw her son he was covered in her blood, a fallen scrap of meat. Her tongue was a fat dry worm in her mouth, numb as the rest of her. She did not want him. She was fifteen years old: she wanted the stuffed pink pony from her bedroom at home, she wanted to go back to school, she wanted her mother.

Her son in the nurse's arms was cat-sized, swaddled, his face patty-pan flat and dark as a bruise. You have to take him eventually, the nurse said. He needs to eat. And she thought, *What does that have to do with me?*

Checks come twice a month: the last Monday from the hospital and the last Friday from the state. That first week after she cashes them is Christmas, is a birthday party, is the Fourth of July. She goes to the grocery store and the liquor store and she takes a bus and a shuttle to the outlets, twenty miles south on the highway. The mall in town is dead. The last store closed in 2010 and now the brick veneers are crumbling away from the cinderblock walls beneath, the walkways chewed through with goldenrod. There's a 3D theater at the outlet mall, an optometrist and podiatrist and minute clinic. There's a nail spa and hair salon and a Mexican restaurant with five kinds of salsa and eight flavors of Margarita. The drinks come in heavy blue glasses with cactus arms sprouting from the thick stems. There's nothing like them in town, and every month she sits at a table by the window, her Dollar Store bags in a shiny plastic pile on the chair next to her, and orders a different kind. So far she hasn't liked any of them, not the mango or the kiwi or the other strange flavors – how could fruit be so *sour?* – but she drinks them anyway, looking out over the parking lot to the shuttle stop, her eye on the clock over the door, free chips and salsa slicking the paper-lined basket with grease.

There are the checks and then there's the other money, the tens and twenties on a Tuesday night, creased, used soft; sometimes a fifty but not often. There are things she won't do anymore, and things they can't afford, and if they run short sometimes of cash she'll accept a different currency: drinks are money, and egg rolls from the Chinese place by the gas station. A fresh pack of cigarettes, lottery tickets, a ride home through the wolf-jawed cold.

• • •

Saturday night and here they are, Roy and his mother and June, the bartender, waitresses, giggling girls and blank-faced men, all of them in a too-loud room strung with smoke-stained paper spiders left from Halloween. Outside the wind hisses and sings; outside bare branches shake.

Inside is a different story. The windows are fogged with drunken laughter and the steam from the glass washer under the bar, and if this place is not exactly safe it's shelter enough – no one, tonight, will cry or rage or bleed here. That will happen later, when their own doors lock behind them.

Roy and his mother will not see each other. When she shoulders the door open June has Roy's face in her powdery hands, her fingers dusting over his cheeks and lips and eyelids, and his mother, heedless, pushes through the square tables and gouged wooden chairs to the bar, slides sideways onto an empty stool. Between them the air churns, spilled beer and struck matches, and waitresses carry red plastic trays of soft pretzels and French fries above the roil. The older men stare imperturbable into their drinks and the younger ones aim their smiles at the girls who sit in twos and threes, pink cheeks damp and knees jittery, unsteady hands cupped around their lighters' nervous flames.

Roy's mother sorts through the scraps of paper in her purse while she waits for the bartender to mix her drink. Check stubs, receipts, the hospital schedule in color-coded triplicate, Powerball scratch-off cards: days and dollars annotated and recorded, incremental, unrelenting. The girls next to her shriek with sudden laughter and grab with oblivious fingers at each other's shoulders, and when the bartender brings Roy's mother's drink they lean across the bar, damp-eyed and gasping, to cry for another round.

June and Roy are side by side in a booth, her legs curled under her and her skirt tucked around them like a blanket, drinks and cigarettes and sticky menu cards on the table. She kisses his neck and tugs her sleeves down over her hands before picking up her glass so that the only skin he can see is her face and fingertips. The rest of her is cocooned in wool, amorphous, indistinct. She is the opposite of naked and his cock is on fire.

Roy pays their tab as his mother starts hers and June slips out of the booth, shoulders her bag and turns for the door. Roy's mother hunches over her glass, pinches the straw with two fingers and sips. He watches June, the pale cloud of her hair swirled and staticky over her shoulders, her skirt hanging uneven and the heels of her boots worn. He would almost recognize her more easily from behind, given how used he is to looking at her back: when she crabs her way up from the river and he follows with rod and fish and creel; when she sits reading at the table while he cooks for her at the stove against the wall. He even fucks her from behind.

Outside it's all he can do to keep from pushing her against the cinderblock wall and shoving her skirt up, his face in her dandelion hair, one hand on her doll-stitched neck and the other between her legs, working them open, her skin glitter and dust, all of her stubborn singularity under his calloused palms.

. . .

Roy's mother signals the bartender before she's finished her first drink and he nods. She's not a regular here but she may as well be. She'll give it another round, two at most, before moving on. The crowd tonight is young, the girls already getting sloppy and the men – hardly more than boys – already taking notice. There's nothing for her here but more obsolescence.

They used to go shopping, she and her mother and Uncle Al before he left. The last time was a trip to Penney's, the cosmetics counter for perfume for her mother and the juniors department for her, for bell-bottoms with patch pockets and a mother-of-pearl crescent moon on a silver chain. The walls of the store were bubblegum-pink, ecstatic with looping neon graffiti. Uncle Al opened his wallet and rifled through credit cards like a magician.

She lifts her chin, presses her tongue to the roof of her mouth to smooth her throat, arranges her face in what she hopes is a serene smile, and waits. Fate: anyone could come in. Destiny: it's just a matter of being ready.

The bartender sets her new drink down and takes her empty glass away. It's an investment, this drink, she thinks; a physical manifestation of her optimism. She has never had a credit card in her life but neither has she ever gone without – electricity, food, a winter coat – she has gone with less, with used, with old, but not without.

You have to think of it as insurance, Uncle Al used to say to her mother. You have to visualize the best possible scenario and then you plan for that. You can't be afraid to borrow against future successes. Do you get me?

Outside the snow begins, not flakes but blowing icy bits, and Roy's mother clasps her hands neatly around her glass. Her fingers are dry and cracked at the knuckles and her nails are chewed but they are warm, her hands, and that's all that will matter when someone ducks in from what's coming.

• • •

Roy follows June from the truck over the slick of mud and freezing grass. He reaches around her to key the front door open and when he does she slips through it as though the house has sucked her, frantic, into itself.

He could kick the door off its hinges. Instead he eases it closed behind him, stomps his boots on the towel just inside. She's already dropping layers of clothes where she stands, crouching to stretch her fingers out to the dog who's inching toward her, haunches stiff and shaking, nose quivering at her feet. She looks up to him and smiles, radiant, the scars around her mouth and eyes dimpling, and the thought that one day she won't be here is a barbed hook in his chest.

He can count to twenty in Spanish, French, German. He can name every Tudor king. He knows the difference between simple future and future perfect.

He isn't stupid: he understands how little he knows and how much less it matters.

• • •

Roy's mother raises a delicate finger to the bartender, who nods and turns toward the register. When he tucks the tab beneath her glass of melting ice she sees he hasn't charged her for one drink, two, four? It's after midnight and she lost track hours ago. He watches her without pretending not to – it's his job, after all. He watches everyone.

She stands, unsteady for only a minute, fishes a five dollar bill from her purse and that fast he's in front of her, shaggy-haired and broad-shouldered. His collar is ironed and clean. Someone's son. Not hers.

Not so fast, someone's son says to her, eyes crinkling with something close to kindness. He lays his big hand on hers, on the money, on the check. You've had a lot to drink, he says, and it's true so why would she argue? A lot more than it says there – he nods toward her hand under his, squeezes it, and she is neither drunk enough to misunderstand nor sober enough to explain that this was not the transaction she had planned, when she came in earlier; not one she would have agreed to had she been given a choice instead of drink after drink, each more expensive than the last. His hand presses into hers, inexorable as winter.

She sits again, defeated. It's futile to argue with this night's cold economy, which, she understands even now, she was never in a position to determine. None of them are, not the perfumed slurring girls next to her or the men with oil-stained leather wallets in their hip pockets: they are all of them playing the best hand they have. She looks around the room and is filled with compassion, and is filled with rage.

• • •

Roy fills the dog's bowls and June forks potatoes from the pan on the stove, pinches strips of dried venison and tears at them with her teeth. He could feed her anything, he thinks sometimes, staghorn sumac and chokeberries, stinging nettle from his fingers. He can picture her stripping bark from the trees with her vampire teeth, digging for grubs with those hands.

The dog snaps and noses the bowl across the floor. Outside the wind pulls the clouds apart and in the distance town rattles and pants, wakes itself to watch for the coming nothing. June licks her fingers, stretches her arms wide overhead and Roy presses his lips into the skin beneath, into the raised purple twists along her ribcage.

They gave me fade cream when they discharged me but I lost it, she says, tilting her hips into him, gripping his waist with her knees, and her skirt is ripped at the seams, the boy's undershirt she wears instead of a bra is yellowing along the neckline. He cups her ass in his hands and wonders did she wear clothes like this before him, before here; did she bother to comb her hair, to wash?

She tastes like wet earth and dry leaves, like carnage. The dog whines at her bare feet. It can smell how soon she'll be gone.

She says I think I want to stay here.

She says But I don't think I can.

Venison on her lips and Roy can taste the deer, shot, hoisted and secured then split, hot guts spilling lavish on the ground. The house is different with her in it.

He understands, for the first time since June has been with him, that he will be relieved when she goes, when he will no longer have to wonder when or how it will happen. He understands that her absence will last longer and so become sweeter than her presence, and for a second he almost wants to hurry her toward her leaving, toward the the door that will close between *before* and *after*.

Almost.

Her skin is slippery under his hands; it smells of sandalwood, sweat and resin. She hooks her arms around his neck and her legs around his waist for him to carry her to the bedroom, to the unmade bed with the sheets bunched and dirt-smudged at the bottom. He drops her there and turns her facedown, her hair matted and damp on her neck and the soles of her feet dirty as a child's. He kneels over her and catches both wrists above her head with one hand, works at the zipper of his pants with the other and the bed will never be wider than it is right now, the house will never be warmer, town will never be farther away.

Even if I never leave this place someone will know I was here.

. . .

Simple future: Roy's mother will be found among the vertebral rocks, face up on the root-split earth, cracked white sky above her.

Future perfect: She will have been there for days.

The sheriff knocks on Roy's door before dawn, before the six a.m. local news, before the papers hit driveways and bushes. Roy answers, shivering in a T-shirt, his hand on the blind dog's collar. He listens. He is alone. He is used to it again. It took no time at all. He leaves the sheriff to wait on the frozen grass while he dresses, thermal shirt then flannel, pants and socks and boots, wool cap on his uncombed hair. He sits in the back seat of the cruiser. It's the first time he's been in one. He was a good boy.

The sheriff drives to the hospital where Roy's mother worked three days a week, where June was made not good as new but good enough, where Roy has never had reason to go since he broke an arm at five. He was a good boy.

The sheriff steps ahead and the automatic door sucks open. Roy follows him through the glassed-in vestibule, past the information desk to the elevator bank. The sheriff hits the DOWN button. They wait without speaking. When the elevator comes the sheriff hits the BASEMENT button.

They exit into the low-ceilinged hallway and the sheriff pivots to face him.

I'm going to go in with you, he says. I'm going to stay until you make the identification and then I'm going to wait in the hallway until you finish.

Finish what? Roy thinks, but does not ask.

His mother's face is split fruit, bruised – somehow both gaunt and puffy. Her lips are swollen, grayish – blood dried to black at the corners. The skin beneath her eyes is dark and wet-looking; her forehead shines under the lights. The hair is scraped away from it, copper-bright but dark at the roots.

He remembers the eye-burning smell of hair dye, his mother in the bathroom they shared with her hands in clownish plastic gloves and orange rivulets running down her arms and neck, splattering the sink and wallpaper. It was the night before he started first grade and he was waiting for his bath.

Don't you want all your new teachers to think Mommy's pretty? she said, shooing him out of the bathroom with the toe of her socked foot. *And that nice Mr Jaffert in the office? Go on, let me finish.*

In the morning she knelt in front of him to tie his shoes and her scalp at the part was the color of a tangerine.

It is not yet eight o'clock when Roy steps out of the hospital. The sun is up and bright, the mountain half in shadow and the moon still just visible, a powdery disc on the blue of the sky. The sheriff is behind him now, and Roy can smell the smoke of the cigarette he's just lit on the cold air.

You want to stop back home first or go into town? he says, and Roy understands that this is not, in fact, a choice; there is work to be done, and it must be done now, and no one will do it but him. *Town,* he says, and the sheriff nods, flicks his cigarette onto the parking lot and unlocks the car doors.

The sheriff drives slowly under the peacock sky. There's no hurry. Town is patient as a snake and just as cold.

From the back seat Roy watches the frost sparked by sun on the dead fields, the flap and hop of crows on the cold ground, and wonders if it will look different to him once his mother is in it.

· · ·

In the house that is barely a house Roy wipes the floors down with beeswax and linseed oil, dredges the gutters and re-caulks the windows. He puts chains on the tires of his truck and checks the antifreeze and wiper fluid. He removes the screen from the kitchen door, weather strips the panes and secures the knob to the frame with a bungee. In the bedroom he alphabetizes the paperbacks he's collected from the boxes he finds in parking lots, in driveways.

In the pantry he arranges jars of blackberry and rosehip jam, pickled onions and Jerusalem artichokes. By the time he zips his coat on all that's left of the sun is a crimson lip at the ridgeline, and he flips the floodlights on. They shine directly on the carcass that hangs from the sawtooth behind the bedroom window.

He lays a tarp over the wooden picnic table under the tree, lays out his knife and saw and splitter. He cuts the deer free and heaves her onto the tarp. He breaks her down, shoulders first and velvet neck, ruby loin and haunches. The wind comes in from the west, slow at first and then stronger over the split and silty earth, through the spicebush and rye. He's elbow-deep in her blood. He'll eat the pretty all winter.

Jason Schwartz

Herringbone

I

A gentleman from town, attired in wool, atop a black animal. Children appear at the treeline? Ten of them, or eleven. And they are beguiled by the wide field? They are not. The gentleman, having undertaken to fall, now assumes a loathsome pose in the gloaming.

Just another bedtime story for us at the orphanage – yes?

It concludes in the gallery, where the family – wooden figures, certainly, rather than wax forms – loses two years. Or one year – if we account for the river, and the dumbwaiter, and the excursions to foreign cities. The family wears, for the duration of this period – or at least its earliest, finest portion – mourning. But the widow seems quite cheered, later on, by a blur of dirt on the davenport.

Shall we distinguish such creatures from common statues, vanishing on the plain?

Mannikins of a different character, acting in place of daggers and brackets, as printer's marks – these are no doubt mistaken on occasion for errata or perhaps the remnants of insects. One imagines the margins inhabited by gnats, for instance, aswarm in so-called ghosts – those splendid clouds from which the suitors plummet.

The term also refers to various hinges and rivets, and to a peculiar cylinder – bronze or copper, as the case may be, and resembling a slender finger or a dwindled man. Other mannikins resemble timbers or stanchions – likely in a very poor light indeed – or wagon-tongues in the countryside, trembling dreadfully.

The gentleman – a certain William, a Mr Hall – is delivered safely to his grave. While a Mr Anderson, one century hence, is replaced in his – by a sack of rats, cinched with a segment of wire. We need not dwell upon the vivid particulars of his affliction. Or the mischief that consigns his remains to a farm cart, travelling around a mountain and through a valley, a brown thorn – to borrow the parlance – captured at the city gate.

But another grave, a better one, may contain a mannikin in lieu of the body. Or perhaps the grave exhibits an ordinary portrait, drawn on the coffin floor. The coffin bell, in such cases, is no doubt absent its tongue – a surmise that does call to mind those wartime stories from the north, in which the victim hangs within a church bell. It is upon us, then, to consider the belltower and the wind – if not the timbre of the man, by this hour or the next, his hat having managed a rather extravagant descent.

When we define the mannikin – in distinction to, say, the lay figure or the tailor's dummy – we count sixty digits, or stitches, from throat to feet. At least in some renderings – superbly alert, as they are, to the obligations of the occasion. And at some country houses, where pins have been arranged into clockfaces – or hidden within the limbs.

The gentleman's possessions burn in the boxroom – as we escort a silhouette through the door and then make gracelessly away. The family, thereupon, withdraws to the lawn, or explores the meadow, or collapses at the shoreline. Or simply returns home to its ruin – despite the ornate pattern on the scrap, for instance, and the small misfortune on the windowsill.

Window sorrow, incidentally, is a variety of ivy – darkening the glass, yes, and sometimes conjuring bodies in the vines.

But these notions fail to explain the condition of the miniatures. One imagines wooden figurines in wooden crates – transported from foreign cities, and presented to the children in wintertime. Here is Katherine, in agony, evidently strangled by a fragment of houndstooth. Poor Nora, of course, in the company of termites, arrives without eyes – or, less likely, as a bundle of sawdust.

Gentlemen, it would seem, always have ten mouths, apparent on their garments as ten gashes, north to south.

Household mannikins – parlor dolls, to be exact – might adorn a chaise or an armchair. Notice the likeness to certain late relations. Porcelain effigies are hidden behind a curtain – as tradition insists. Cloth effigies – impeccably red – are carried into battle on horseback, and sometimes posed among bones on the forest floor.

Common worms in the garden – these are accidents of grammar, according to one early lexicon. An addendum refers to black stains of a particular shape, replacing the faces in family portraits. Mannekins –

or mannikens, a less remote variant – are figurations in wrought iron, in cornice patterns, in grim brown traceries. Imperfections, clearly enough – rather than, say, codes or omens. Manakins, for their part, are birds of the New World, frightfully small. We might mistake them for finches or wrens or, more crudely, hands in the grass – with a treeline as the margin of the scene.

II

But manakins are absent from the ballroom, even in the afternoon. Ten vitrines in neat arrangement? An improvement, at any rate, over the cartons of pigeons. And the wrens inhabit a pipe organ? Perhaps a cannon on the lawn. The blunderbuss – discovered on the post road – is constructed of branches, twine, and glass.

You can fashion a napkin into a hand – or into a bird of some kind, now bleeding at your feet.

False birds, so-called, are carved of wood, and scattered in yards and fields – creating, it would seem, false maps for travellers. Compare them with these clever anatomies, pen-and-ink – in which birds occupy the stations of the organs. A sensible explanation, then, for the shrike – very much alive – woven inside a child's ribcage in 1412, replacing the heart.

Schoolboys – two or three of them, and later eight or nine, attired in finery – play statues every Saturday, atop black houses. Such facts, naturally, cannot account for the petrified gentlemen at the fenceline – or, for that matter, the petrified sparrows on the wire, said to have been beheaded by the wind.

Prisoners are beheaded in the arbor, the bodies displayed beside a pond. In the memory, anyway, of a Mrs Nicholas, travelling the mountains by carriage and wagon. A jackdaw, attending to the flesh, might indeed be mistaken – from this great distance, and at that hour – for a crooked face. Elsewhere, of course, martins are tethered to skeletons, replacing the skulls. The rags – per the terms of a common holiday frolic – are set afire in the square.

Even the weathervane claims acquaintance with a red shape – or a wretched outline in a riverbed.

The dimensions of the manakin – shown at the bottom of the column, in fly's-eye – are incorrect, as expected. The names summon cheerless scenes. Clockwise, if you please – the specimens in distress, and under glass, and dismantled. But the smallest form – an approximation, keenly realized, in metal and wool – adorns a lapel.

A Miss Watt, for her part, wears a velvet hat, affixed to which a single rail – disembarrassed of its innards, and stuffed with cotton batting. This – thoroughfare, avenue, bridge – is not, perhaps, the most exquisite route. Despite evidence of a Mrs Hall, wearing a straw hat, somewhat later in the year – the blackbirds preserved in standard fashion, and impaled on a painted branch.

You might prefer, under the circumstances, red skirts – but you discover, instead, curtains burning in the windows.

The sounds of the manakin – these, at least – are gray marks on walls and doors. Superstition no doubt accounts for the silver plateau, as well – reflecting claws, it would seem, from the teapot. It shivers, the bird. But the call suggests neither the gasp nor the wail of, say, a melancholy man. The notes rise twice – as in certain other species – and then die quite slowly.

The sounds of the riflebird, by contrast, suggest gunfire – explaining the name, quaintly, to a family in the landscape. The color, in porcelain versions, is evidently a happy distraction – or a simple lapse of manners. Consider, likewise, the formation of persons in lonesome poses, set upon by jackals and lions in a tapestry pattern. The bird is mistaken, in this case, for a bright letter at the throat.

The diagrams – or remnants thereof – exhibit the organs in cross section. But the gullet and lungs are always absent – subject to the ravages, the caption reads, of one antique disease or another. The exploded bird, in turn, arranges its elements at dismal angles, with several cursive phrases – unless these are rows of sawteeth – decorating the edge of the page.

Wolves, drawn on cloth, are found in a garden, hidden among the ferns. Rattlebirds hang from the barn roof. Scarecrows – or a commotion of posts and beams, attired in ratcatcher – replace children on the hillside. Their costumes – antlers and tails, and plaster masks – are now in piles beneath the trees.

As for the ghastly shadows on the glass – these are just branches, after all, unsettled by the weather.

The pigeons, anyway, are gone – forsaken or lost in a corner of the forest. They are named, according to older notations, for a mishap with an ax. Wrens are named – and here a gentleman acts rather a tragic part – for a form of contagion. Their footprints are often thought a code of sorts. Manakins – and mannikins, an Eastern variety – are said to resemble wounds, as you might assume. The name is from the Dutch – 'little man' – by way of a body in misery. It is displayed in a field, or so the story goes – the eyes quite distant from their sockets, and the mouth pinned shut.

III

Children fall at the treeline. Ten of them – prone – or perhaps eleven. Shall we consider their attire? Unfortunate – in light of later events. And the birds in the dirt? These are finches, naturally, rather than manakins. The pattern in the background – an unseemly gray – now suggests houses and a town.

I would hide – supine, as I recall – in a blue room.

The cabinet – which exhibits, in this instance, fifteen rooms – stands across from the davenport. We begin with the gentleman – third floor, west end – in his desolation, and conclude with the family – ground floor, hallway – in its terror. Which does neglect, however, the animal on the balcony – apparently crestfallen, or merely forlorn.

The scale, in general, is one inch to the foot – such that the objects, at night, may summon for us various memories, dire and otherwise.

And summon for a Mrs Anderson – in her years, at table with a plate of rancid bear – a modicum of regret. The black specks, at any rate, are magnificent – their reflections suggesting ants in transit, crossing from one implement to the next. The napkin – not at all torn – carries a green monogram, ring stitch.

The relic is a segment of red thread, of the kind once found – at the hem, as a device or a sign – in burial dresses. It appears, therefore, within a miniature coffin – rather as the splinter inhabits a miniature house. The bone, or what remains of it, discolors the lower jaw – the bust encased within a square of glass. The captions are exaggerations – or, less plausibly, common ravens.

But if the windowpanes are replaced with persons – we might then discover, with some profit, a better portion of the garment.

It was – forgive me – a woollen shirt of no great distinction. I wore it as a boy.

The earliest mannikins – at least as they occur in certain ungracious translations – are small flaws in the scenery. Or, if you like, tiny mistakes in the landscape. A single fore-edge, perhaps – executed in blue, and absent several pages. The burnt spots are called foxes. But the split tongue is not always a hurt bird – obscured, in part, by an ornament or a name. And the corpses – which may very well disguise the hillside and the sky – have now simply vanished.

Invisible children, in turn, are commonplace in locket portraits. At the border, right side – or left side, as the case may be. The orphans in cross section, and the family in cutaway – these creatures, unhappily, have forgotten all about Blanche and Mary. The hidden mother – a Mrs Hearne, this time; a Mrs Flint, the next – holds the child in a tintype, the curtain drawn from ceiling to floor.

I attempted, shall we say, a most exemplary pose – at the garden wall, too late in the afternoon.

The smallest mannikins are captured – or entombed, as some narratives have it – behind schoolroom walls, in miniature towns. The bottle dungeon, so-called, assumes a human shape, eight feet deep. The valise – now in the possession of the gentleman – has a false bottom, within which several narrow pockets, the lining quite torn. While the pigeonholes, it turns out, contain only feathers and claws.

A fragment of the gullet – magnified one hundred times – exhibits wires in a kind of stitchery, curiously decorative in effect. Which is not to claim for it, however, a likeness to fire – though the bacterium, on an ivory slide, does quiver prettily enough. Various misadventures, after all – from the cottage to the village, and back again – as the lungs fill with blood.

The deer hooves are torches, per a different report – which presents, as well, an arrangement of ruined costumes.

The cabinet was black. But the wardrobe had a gray floor – rather poorly adorned, I am afraid.

The hidden mannikins – charming figures in the wilderness, heads severed – may recall certain effigies, buried at the treeline. Or perhaps the gentleman at his catastrophe – throat slit on parchment. In minium – red, that is to say – as distinct from minum, which simply conjures the mantel clock. The zero, of course, appears in another color. The grave doll – formed according to the facts of the malady – hangs on the nursery wall. While the child in the cupboard – too neatly concealed, alas – is transported north as a corpse.

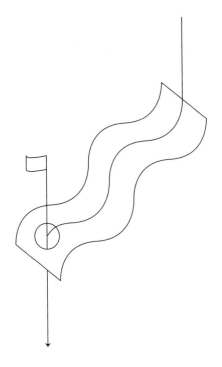

Kathryn Scanlan

Two Fictions

DEAR SIRS

Dear Sirs, I am writing to you this morning because I very much admire your products and am desiring to make a purchase of them. I have made my selections from the many different options available to me, and am now prepared to pay you the requisite monies. Believe me, it was not an easy decision. For you have so many wonderful products, I have a hard time choosing. The first time I saw your products, I could not help but shouting! They bring me joy and I feel exclusively warm from those. I could not put them from my mind. I would think of how good it would be to own them and to look at them every day in the comfort of my own home. My home is no doubt very small by your standards and it is maybe not as comfortable as one would like, especially one accustomed to the very great comforts you are no doubt in possession of – however, for me it is comfortable enough, and because I do not move around much, the smallness does not impinge upon me the way it doubtless would impinge upon you, Sirs. One might think it too small to contain even a single one of your products – no less the several of them I am hoping to purchase today – however, I can assure you I have taken great pains to clear a space within which the full excellence of your items will be easily apprehended by all who chance to look on them, although in truth I rarely entertain guests due to the smallness of my home as I have mentioned, and it will most likely be myself only who feasts his eyes. But a man must have his private pleasures, mustn't he? I said to myself, You cannot bring these into your home without having first prepared for them a good place, a nice place. You would not bring home a new baby without first having made for it a little bed laid with soft blankets and something special for it to look at, something you've hung from the ceiling to catch the light of the sun, because you know babies need this type of enchantment. And so I have worked hard and made many sacrifices, but now the day has finally come.

My problem at this moment, Sirs – and the reason I write to you this morning – is that I cannot find my country. I have completed the questions you ask of me – for example my full name and the street on which I reside – however, in perusing the list of countries you so generously provide, from which I am to choose, I do not see my own. I see you have ordered the countries in an alphabetical arrangement. This is good and helpful and I thank you for your consideration! However, in the location where my country should rightfully reside, I find only the country before it and the country after – alphabetically speaking. It appears my country has gone missing. I see no other explanation for it. I see the names of many, many other countries here listed. Some are very great countries, the very best ones. Yours, for example, good Sirs. But there are many lesser countries represented here as well – many, even, that are very bad. I hope you will not think me too bold when I say that my own country

– small though it may be – is far superior to many of these very low and bad places to be found on your list. And yet, they are there and we are not. I think to myself, perhaps it is because of our smallness – for indeed we are very small here, smaller than most – that we cannot be found. Perhaps we are so small, you have forgotten us? If you have indeed forgotten us – an oversight I comprehend easily, being myself a servant in a clerical capacity who is tasked daily with many a trivial detail, who is forever failing to remember some item or other of little import to myself yet significant, even gravely so, to some other party, it never fails to surprise me, these matters of life or death with which I am charged, so often without my full realization, so rarely aware of the individuals involved, and of the consequences of this pen stroke or that – I say, if indeed you have forgotten us, I here humbly submit my request. At your earliest convenience, and barring any unforeseen and comprehensible reason as to why you would not, might you attend to – nay, rectify – the situation as outlined above, in which I, together with my countrymen – a good and clean people we – have been made to wait, so many of us, until such time as you deem it appropriate?

Next door was a diner that burned bread and scalded coffee. Its exhalations – like the breath of an elderly relative on your cheek – arrived each morning and staled into afternoon.

Mondays, my colleague brought a large, foil-wrapped casserole of canned biscuit, hot dog, and boxed egg substitute, topped with shredded cheese. He stored it in the refrigerator and microwaved a portion for lunch each day until, on Friday evening, he carried the empty, heavily crusted dish home with him – presumably to be soaked over the weekend before the ritual could begin again.

I kept a package of imported butter to cut in thick, cold slabs onto seeded crackers. I ate radishes when I had them, or sometimes an apple or cucumber. I poured salt onto my palm and tongued it into my mouth. The rubbery tumblers were permanently perfumed by the purple dish soap, so I leaned my head instead to drink straight from the tap.

• • •

My colleague dragged boxes of tubes from back to front, where he affixed stickers to plastic caps and secured the caps to the ends of the tubes. He used a compressed air gun that shot small, thick staples. Depending on how he held it, the gun said, *That's it, that's it, that's it!* or *Stop it, stop it, stop it!*

I cut open other boxes and distributed their contents. My cutter was a good one, and like the better pens and sharper scissors, it wound up often on my colleague's desk. I retrieved things when he ate his lunch. I disarranged his papers and other items to demonstrate my irritation, but from what I could tell, he was an individual accustomed to disorder, and did not notice.

• • •

We wore tiny speakers in our ears plugged to devices in our pants, but mostly I listened to what came from his – thin crashing, faint wailing: a thimble-sized man in a seashell, raging.

He was moody, and his mood could alter the temperature and barometric pressure of the room. He'd come in with it rising from him like a stink – a sullen yellow sulk that soured as the day wore on. He kicked boxes and table legs and slammed doors. He banged dishes in the sink. He sighed heavily – often.

He smoked cigarettes in the alley with the man who lived behind our dumpster, in an alcove that abutted the small, frosted window of our bathroom. Sometimes I'd see this man pushing a cart loaded with items – brisk and businesslike as a busy mother at the bulk discount store.

I'm free, I heard the man say to my colleague.

I want to be free, my colleague said. Then came the metallic crack of his lighter and a sharp intake of breath.

• • •

My colleague was slender but wore loose pants and shirts which made him seem larger. Around his neck hung a fine gold chain with a pendant he kept tucked from sight – a small lump on his chest. Once, when he leaned over, it slipped out and swung in the open a moment. It may have been an animal or domestic object like an iron or frying pan, the sort you see chained to the wrist of a woman who has collected or been given these small, gold-plated representations of her life to wear.

A bracelet like that was purchased for me by the women of my family when my body announced its bloody ability to make a human child. On schoolroom desktops, the bracelet clanged and clunked.

My narrative expanded to include an ice skate, a horseshoe, a terrier, a baseball mitt, a pencil, an apple, a long-haired cat, a book, a bicycle, a piano, a graduation cap, and an ice cream cone.

I sold it to a man at a junk shop and bought a matinee movie ticket. At the climax, the woman forsook her modest pantsuit for something tight and leathery. She let a grotesque banker molest her and she allowed a fat attorney strike her with the butt of a gun. But in the end the woman got what she wanted and was happy.

• • •

Then – how can I explain it? One day, requiring something, I handed my colleague a sheet of paper and pointed. Please, I said. That rusty old word – I expelled it like a clot of phlegm from my wheedling childhood.

When he reached for the paper, his hand touched mine. From the clammy point of impact, a wild jolt careened up my arm – straight to the hollow holding tanks of heart and brain.

The gold chain glittered above the grubby collar of his shirt. The skin there was florid, taut. I watched my hand rise toward it. Then I jerked back and patted the hair on my head instead. He didn't notice – or maybe he did.

Whatever you need, he said.

• • •

Near the end, when my colleague was out on an errand, someone knocked. It was not a door people came to but I went and listened. I heard an impatient sound from a man's throat.

Who is it? I said.

I have a package, said the man.

I opened the door. The man's face was ugly and his hands were empty. He stuck his heavy booted foot into the gap. He laid a hand on the frame and leaned in.

What exactly goes on here? he said.

Behind him, my colleague pulled up and parked his car. He'd spray-painted it himself, black and white, like a spectator shoe – a style I've never found attractive. Dazed, freckle-faced, he came toward us carrying a plastic sack – a slight, sloppy, slouching boy with an unformed face, a backwards cap, an undone sneaker. It's how I think of him now, when I think of him.

The man looked back and I grabbed the small, dust-grimed fire extinguisher the owners set near the door on our first day. I brought it into solid contact with the man's shin.

The man screamed. He hobbled, doubled-over. Briefly he fell to one knee. Then he surged up, bellowing like a cow. He grabbed my colleague by the neck and pinned him against the building. I got behind the man and struck his ass with my foot. My colleague fluttered his hands, buffeting the man's face with soft slaps until he got hold of the nose with the heel of his palm and pushed it up – snout-like.

Motherfucker, I said quietly as I kicked.

Then, abruptly, the man let go. He stepped back. He wiped his nose, inspected the smear. He brushed his clothes with quick, stiff strokes. Then he shoved his hands in his pockets and – with a limp – walked away. Halfway down the block, he began to whistle. It was a song everyone knew but no one, to my knowledge, liked.

My colleague leaned, hands on knees, and wheezed. I picked up the plastic sack from where he'd dropped it and found the pack of cigarettes inside. I unwrapped it and thumped it twice, hard, on my hand.

Cigarette? I said.

Yes, he said.

After that came the period I will describe as our golden age, which lasted about as long as any era of comparable improbability.

Russell Persson

Lyric Suite

Allegretto gioviale

In the first movement, Alban learns the bones who run inside himself the bones who spoken together make up inside him the tallness he was given these bones who have the next day holed up inside him in the coral mud of them it is Alban learns his bones would change. He first learned his bones were in him. Then Alban learns his bones would change and this is in night. He is in bed in night and it is warm up on the second floor even with the shutters open and there are bug sounds in odd cadence outside and he is in bed in the notice of the pain his creaking stretching bones are up to in him.

He didn't know his bones would change. In night inside him where his sounds began their courses into music where from in his bones the bars would come and him along the bars go dotted in the notes who came from in him he knew his bones were the fund of him but he didn't know his bones would change.

If his bones, he imagines in night his racing night, fell into the floor of his bag down in the shins and inside his ocean feet, the click of all this would be like the three notes of the bug outside who beats three times and in the final notes of this first movement those bugs who run in threes collect the sound of fallen bones they come apart and drum down to the bag the floor.

Andante amoroso

The second movement begins at the Berghof near the Ossiarcharsee in Carinthia. Upstairs Alban lies in bed and in the summer it is warm upstairs and so his bedroom windows are open the shutters folded into the room and collapsed against the window frames and from outside his open windows are the crickets and the sounds of crickets and the small sick birds who carry the crickets off through the weeds and the tall grass and there is also the sound of the wind and what the wind becomes inside the leaves outside his window what the leaves become with the wind inside them and all this along with the hum inside Alban this hum which is his excess his engine who can not stop or settle in night his excess his seventeen years come to this in night him unslept and lively. The zest and unsettle his bones are a part of him and this all builded in his bones and from there spoken as one who hums is never alone for the always of it. Spoken like a color of light and ember.

Downstairs on the floors below him only them who serve inside the Berghof are still about arranging things back to where and he is awake for no certain cause other than his own excess still runs about inside him with a blue and grown avast who needles out from in him and sets him up awake in night.

Allegro misterioso – Trio estatico

In the third movement she comes to him and he is un–
contained and in his excess. He is already rigid and he
thinks ahead to when she turns the handle of the door
with an evening hand. She comes to him and with her
she will bring herself and how she enters and he is un–
contained.

In night she comes to him a quiet hand to let her in
and she closes the quiet door behind her. She has with
her a pitcher of water and the candle she blows out
and sets the sterling candlestick on top of his wooden
dresser. She crosses the room the wool rug and sets the
pitcher on his bedside table. He can smell her now and
she smells of what she washed after the dinner and of
the paraffin and lemon she rubs into the dining room
table after the plates have been cleared when she's
alone to clean.

She takes a corner of his bedsheet and pulls it from
off him and he is rigid and a chill runs through him
even for the summer night and it's warm still in his
room but his uncontain sets a coldness in him and he
tries to master himself against the shiver who arrives.
Get up and stand over there is what her open hand says
to him. With Alban standed now and his rigid standed
out from him he watches her remove her apron and sit
down on the bed her eyes come up to meet his and she
keeps her eyes remained on his and removes her shoes
and stockings and stands to remove her skirts who fall
down to the wool rug and she removes what was un–
derneath her skirts her eyes remained on his and what

was underneath her skirts falls now to the wool rug and floor. Turning her back to him and lifting her hair it is then Alban sheds the rug the room between them and unfastens what has her dressed yet to fall it to the floor. The moon lends its gray light down on Marie as she sits back down on the bed and lays herself back her eyes remained she sets herself into the middle of his narrow bed the moon itself is trusted and she fixes him down to her so that the same moon is on them both at once a window open and she contains him down to where and she contains him in her steady school.

The final notes are something of a dwindle, the music of it unmoored and under way and becoming more distant and less defined as a face becomes a different face in the almost true dark and there is only the smallest angle of light up along the visage and it turns from one into another and it's only guessed what mood is carried and before the shape is well sussed a scattering comes and the low almost inaudible notes blow off the bow to die off on each a several and small path.

Adagio appassionato
It is described in the fourth movement that the Berg family calls her Mizzi, an informal play on Marie. Mizzi goes to Alban's room in night to fuck him to not so much speak with him but to be with him and she lends her past to these evenings and he begins to learn her maps and wake. She lends the gray shapes of what has come about her over her the bodies she has

known they've come to her before, before Alban. The hard men who rushed and the quiet one who arrived on himself and there was one who was amused it remains on her like the borders and the lines who draw the story of a hillside. In Alban Mizzi finds a dear study an upstairs boy the young Alban with his fuck out racing ahead of him and shy of any measure. She wants to fold him twice, like a sheet, when a sheet is even and less hot. Then unfolded and gathered in her own fuck.

Presto delirando – Tenebroso

In the fifth movement we come to find Alban who walks a path by the Ossiarcharsee in Carinthia with himself along a path who is enough in width for just himself and worn down to the dirt by others who walk here in the shaded wooded stretch and later where the path goes closer to the water and the edge of land against the lake. On clouded days and when the wind is at its least down at the water he can see into the depths where at a slant even then the deepness goes beyond his seeing and what continues under there beyond his seeing is beyond all knowing and contains there a possible key to what all else is unlit. These near vases of what's dark we can just walk down to along the path who leads him from the Berghof to the Ossiarcharsee.

He constructs a quick obituary. After failing school young Alban sunk himself below a lake in summer. His shoes were found by the shore and a search for a farewell letter turned up only a few leaves.

By the lake there is no one in wait and nothing or no one to wait for and so when he is stray as such from the lines who lead him back to them he becomes stray himself and settles into where there is no watch or any question. Loosed upon nothing he hears the wind and across the lake when it is still a voice carries over from the far side and then a bird.

His mother at the Berghof in her own new stillness. It is said our elders see to themselves as they've seen to us.

Largo desolato
In the sixth and final movement Alban is thirty-nine and a respected composer living in the Hietzing district of Vienna with his wife Helene and their housekeeper Anny Lenz. There is an afternoon in Hietzing when Helene is away on a cure and a young woman arrives unannounced to the Berg residence to request permission to take a photograph of the composer. Alban invites the young woman inside. A portrait on the street is unbecoming and indoors a better setting can be arranged. Inside, the young woman reveals herself to be Albine, the daughter of Alban and Marie Scheuchl, Mizzi.

'Because of her beautiful bone structure, she sat for Hans Domenig's "Muttergottesstatue", a Madonna and child sculpture.' – Pat Bamford-Milroy, Grete Kocher

In the final bars of the sixth movement, Alban, fifty years old, having just written a violin concerto in memory of and dedicated to Manon Gropius, forever skeptical of doctors and obsessed since youth by the number twenty-three, is bitten by a winged insect and does not have the infection treated and a few weeks later Alban dies, in the final notes of the Lyric Suite, on December 24, 1935.

Catherine Foulkrod

The Contagious Abortion of Cattle

1917, USA

They called it the Bacillus abortus of Bang, no joke.
Stockmen and dairymen shot up in the night to a
pounding at the door, a light on in the barn. The disease was a killer, an unborn calf killer, second in wrath
only to tuberculosis. Monetary losses were enough to
make a family, the farm, the whole county go under.
The spread was fast enough to show a man he had no
control.

Fetuses and the accompanying discharge were
burned, buried, or both. An onlooker might spit on
the ground against the curse. A hand on the ranch
would perform douches. This is how that job pro-
gressed: iodine, potassium iodide, boiled water, and a
soft rubber tube the length of an arm. There were daily flushes of the uteri despite the cows' protests. The
hand had to be quick because the vulvas clenched.

The bull, too, needed attention. Someone to scrub
its belly and inner thighs. A few men to irrigate its
genitals before and after all intercourse. The weakest
man would direct the hose. The strongest man would
hold back the foreskin with his fists.

In Malta it wasn't Bang, it was Bruce. Same genus (brucella, named after Bruce), different animal (goat). The goats in Malta ran through the streets of Vallaya each morning, thousands of nannies with utters so full they dragged on the ground, got muddied and scraped. A single Maltese goat is enough to nurse a platoon said the men who squatted in the gutters milking, using runoff from one tit to lubricate the next. No refrigeration meant housewives and chefs would ask for refills after lunch. Such was the paradise for the poor and wealthy alike: fresh milk and butter in the morning, cheese and ice cream come afternoon, and an undulant fever that hit peak temperatures after the sun had set. It was an island of sweaty dreams.

Thousands of British troops, not long off the boats from Crimea, drank their milk raw like the locals and soon overflowed the hospitals with shivering and aching bodies. With headaches and backaches and joint aches and homesickness and suicidal calls to Mother. The whores, too, on a street called 'The Gut', showed an upsurge of the bacteria. These women stood their ground in doorways, the fever swaying them like palms.

But it was the monetary threat of so many soldiers in bed – not concern for the women they bedded – that fueled the formation of the eradication team led by Sir Major-General Bruce.

Long history short, Sir Bruce identified the bacterium. His wife was a whiz at the microscope. But the

Major did not attribute much to that wife, nor did he listen to the local doc who realized the fever spread via goat.

Long history longer, eradication took ages. Cooks ordered to boil milk snuck cool liquid into their pots. Diseased goats taken to slaughter were slipped live out backdoors to their original owners. The government even proposed a cow-goat swap, but that was soon aborted. You see, the cows became constipated and their milk tasted like crap.

Condensed milk in cans was the only workable prescription. The military made it protocol and the hospitals dutifully emptied out. The rich folk, too, got hip to cans, thanks to an ad telling them to act more British. But a taste for goats' milk – raw from the source – lingered long within the citizens of Malta. Even as factories sent out sterile milk in electric vans, goats passed between phantom herds across the limestone steppe, evading authorities, spreading the bug.

This is how a middle-aged tourist on a Mediterranean vacation in 1995 ate a savory cheeselet, caught a fever, and died.

They say bacterium is the most abundant form of life. They say the father of microbiology counted more organisms in his mouth than men on the planet. They say antibiotics are no longer working and Russians are reactivating a biological weapon based on Bang's abortus.

They say the milk at the bar is half water, two percent anthrax – that other bacillus. Ninety percent of all genetic material in our bodies is not human, they say. They say we are just a habitat for microbes, a scaffolding, a shell. Women in Beijing, we know, are lactating from super bugs in skyscraper byproducts. Mammal-less milk secreted from GMO yeast was conceived by bacteria in the brains of do-it-yourself scientists. They say bacteria was here first, it came from outer space. Bacterium will be here last, it can now bind to silicon.

But in Sydney it has been officially declared: bacteria are our friends. A larger than life colon is being erected – a monument to how bacteria helps us digest.

Bacteria will be celebrated once a year with wine and sourdough bread. There will be an oil spill in the Gulf of Carpentaria so bacteria can have a feast. The stance in Sydney is not to worry so much. The idea is to whistle while soaping your skin, to sing while rinsing your genitals after sex.

The idea is to drink milk and sleep through the night. Hush now, that light on in the barn is just a bio-luminescent e-coli bulb. That vibration in the earth is only bacteria recomposing new soil. The children may be dirty, but their immune systems are strong. Human newborns suckling peptide-laden milk in the pouches of marsupials are growing at incredible rates.

Robb Todd

Quiet the Remedies

Broken bits of rainbow spin on the walls in every room, and a wooden elephant rolls instead of rocks because this boy, she swears, needs to move, and he scoots across floors and through bending shards of color on the animal she carved, her hair for its lashes.

He will move.

When he is a man, he will move so far away that if he went any farther he would be moving closer, and he never tells her where he is because he feels safer this way, farther and further from her, but never freer of her, and he will come in the face of every woman who will let him and in the face of many who say do not and he will never stop moving, even when he finally stays in one place, and that is where I am.

Here with a different her, a spectrum of hers, and she examines my hand and says, 'Your knuckles look like elephant knees', and I smile and say something while thinking of the tail braided from the same hide as the brass-tack trunk, smooth hips and sanded curves, but bad on corners, no give in the legs, a stampede solo through the sleeping naked room, refracted and washed in evening yolk.

Everything is a prism.

She asks me a question I only ever answer if I gain some advantage from it so I tell her and she cries a little and says, 'I'm so, so sorry', and I know I am not completely being honest. How can anyone ever be completely honest? But she probably wants me a little more because of it, someone to save, and I will let her think she can rescue me.

'I don't know what I'd do without you,' I say. I have a pretty good idea.

We stare at each other sideways, our heads resting on feather pillows. A tear trickles over the bridge where her nose meets her brow and disappears into her other eye, finding its way home. I pluck an eyelash off her cheek, hold it on a fingertip and tell her to make a wish. She has beautiful eyelashes.

'Oh, no!' she says, clamping her hands in front of her chest. 'What if I make the wrong wish?'

The only women who love me are women who hate themselves.

'I don't know which wish to wish for!' she says.

'Just blow,' I say. My eyes narrow and I smile.

'You'd like that,' she says. She closes her eyes and blows. The eyelash sticks to the fingertip.

'Harder,' I say.

'That's my line,' she says, and she blows like she is putting out birthday candles, eyes open, and the eyelash vanishes and I write something down.

She whispers the wish in my ear and her breath does not smell like the breath of other hers, it is her breath, the only wind I want. Everything smells like what it is: fresh hair and flesh. I kiss her and our faces are so close they are blurry, cross-eyed, one-eyed, underwater. I pull away, into focus, and when I stare into a woman's eyes, all I see is my reflection.

I will move.

A man in full colors, who splinters and fades, and she might cry and maybe I will feel bad, but secretly be happy that I can cause so much pain just by not being there.

I do not regret it. I do not regret anything. I regret everything.

'What does it feel like?' I say.

'"What does it feel like?' is my favorite game,' she says. She straddles me, sits up and flips her hair to the side. 'It feels like a stranger staring at you on a train, and you staring back until someone smiles.'

'That's it?' I say.

'It also feels like,' she says, searching for it, 'knee-bows.'

'Ah, now I understand.' I press a finger into my chin. 'I think it feels like a wave right before it crests.'

She purrs and nuzzles my shoulder.

'That's dumb,' she says.

I count the trails of sweat on her chest, eyelashes by the bagful, the hairs on the back of her neck that thinly zipper down her spine. I slide a finger through what is left of me on her skin, close my eyes and memorize her body like a blind man, trace slick lines that glisten against curves and softness and bone. Sentimentality is not free. The cost is being stricken, intertwined.

She rolls off and I open my eyes. A slow, deep bite. A soft moan turns into a whisper, a secret to neither keep nor betray, like the sky in the window, neither day nor night and the lamplight outside flickers, confused.

A passing car fills the room with music and she says, 'The only songs I like are the ones that make me sad or make me want to fuck.'

The music disappears down the street.

'Well,' she says, 'I guess that's kind of the same thing.'

I slap her and she laughs and says it was not hard enough. She is covered with my effort: a bruise like a butterfly wing, another like a bloody kiss under her skin, a crooked ring of red marks, and she wears them like badges and says, 'There's no going back now.'

She has great elbows. I tell her that. Soft, smooth, not too big/small/sharp/dull. Nice. She touches mine and says, 'Wow, you have great elbows, too.' I check. I say, 'Damn, you're right. My elbows are even better than yours. I'm great!' She laughs, probably because it is true. I write that down and she says, 'Write everything down, sir!'

Motorcycles rumble and the windows shake and a bus beeps and hisses at a stop. I count the beeps. Two men yell in another language, words that must be curses and threats.

'See, they know what it feels like, too,' she says, 'because losing it is the only thing that could make anyone that angry.'

I walk to the window to watch the fight but notice an attractive mother in tight jeans holding a tiny hand and I imagine the child being pushed out of her vagina and I imagine the mom being fucked the night of conception and I feel a little bad for thinking about that, or at least for admitting that in my brain there is shit like that.

'This is quite a piece you did on my shoulder,' she says.

A pigeon pecks at something in the street that is so delicious the bird has lost its fear of death. I count the cars that almost hit it and it does not fly out of the way. It just struts to the side, a car barely misses, its feathers ruffle in the whipped air, and it struts back and pecks.

'What happened with those guys?' she says.

The men are gone and I shake my head. Children are playing in the fountain in the park. A plane flies between a star and a silver toenail clipping of day-moon just above the trees and the sky makes the blue it only makes just before dark.

I pull the white leather chair in front of the open window and sit with my back to the world.

'It feels like,' she says, 'a perfectly poached egg.'

A breeze cools my skin and the curtain strokes my face and neck and I close my eyes. All at once: cars honk, motorcycles rev, a bus grumbles, kids, swings, ice cream truck. I open my eyes, swivel in the chair and look out the window. Two baby dolls tied together at the throat hang tangled like shoes from a bowed line over the lit street. To be so close.

'It feels,' I say, 'like a sheet fort.' I really hit the T's. Shee-T. For-T.

She laughs and pulls the sheet over her head and kicks her feet against it until she is out of breath.

'Let's go for a walk,' I say. 'Through the fountain.'

My jeans are crumpled on the floor like the bud of a rose. She tugs her skirt on and I slip into socks and we do little dance moves into the same clothes we wore last night.

Adults and teens and kids still fill the park but the fountain must have been turned off while we got dressed. We are caught in the crossfire of a water-balloon fight.

'Fuck you, nigga!'

'I got one for you, nigga!'

They are not black. Balloons burst. We stay dry. The sky is dark but the clouds are still white. Motor-cycles. Bus breaks. Someone's phone is playing music. We sit on a bench and look at the fountainless fountain. The air is thick. Kids zoom past on bicycles and I feel their wind.

Two guys box next to the monkey bars. Gloves and everything. I want to learn to box, to be boxed. Their gloves pop. I count the pops. Some teens run by, a race. A girl wins. Someone watching says she ran like a jaguar and she did. She beat a boy.

'I'm the fastest nigga around here! Don't forget!' She is not black.

Squeaking playground bridge. Little girls on scoot-ers doing laps: 'When are we going to stop going round and round?'

I write it down and they do another lap.

'Let's go to the boardwalk,' I say.

'It's dark,' she says.

'That's why we should go,' I say. 'We'll ride the roller coaster.'

We walk to the subway station. A kid in a window sprays me with a powerful squirt gun and yells, 'Sorry, mister!' but he does not stop. I am soaked and I yell thanks and I tell the kid that if he knew me at all he would be using bullets.

The spray feels good, chills my face and chest and back. I open my mouth wide and he fills it with water and it is too complicated to drink.

On the train, a baby in a stroller reaches into my wet pocket and tugs at my wallet.

'Aw,' she says.

My feet are puddles. She has never ridden a roller coaster before. She says she is nervous. She bites her lips so much there is a ragged line of flesh on each one. I tell her someone died on the roller coaster recently and she gives me a frightened face. I tell her I will protect her and she kisses me and we make out to the point of annoying other passengers.

She tells me a long story about her archenemy when she was in school. She calls her a whore many times and says, 'I'm sorry. I don't feel like myself. Maybe you won't want to see me again.'

Her lip is bleeding a little from all the chewing and kissing. The train doors slide open and a man says as he leaves, 'Love is amazing with that kiss. Love is amazing! Get a life. Get a life!' I count the people on the train who I think are as unhappy as he is. The baby pulls out my keys and they fall to the floor. I pick them up and the stops roll past.

There is no line for the roller coaster. We have our pick of any seat, front or back. She screams and closes her eyes on the first drop and never stops screaming and she squeezes my arm and I squeeze a boob as we whip around corners alone with the noise, the force of planets stretching our faces.

'Thanks for letting me hold on to you,' she says when we get off. 'That was the best part. I think I may have pissed a little.' She pats her skirt. 'No, I didn't.'

We walk out over the water to the end of a pier. The boards are crooked and nails lift their bent heads. People fish and play music. We kiss again and a little girl walks by and says, 'Somebody eat my eyes.' I write that down.

I lean over the railing and watch the water lap against wood pimpled with barnacles and mussels and I spit and watch the white dots disappear in a swirl. She spits, too.

'It's only fair,' she says and she makes a mock-stern face. I write something down and she says, 'Taking notes!'

The ocean wind echoes in my ear and waves are better than music, and reels click and spin and birds cry and lines are cast and children squeal on the beach. We walk past carnival games and freak shows and beggars and cotton candy on the boardwalk and a little boy with wild hair wins a stuffed elephant, big enough for him to sit on, and he does an the knees give. A fake palm tree in the sand sprays rainbow mist under the boardwalk lights, and I walk into it to hide the water welling in my eyes and she follows me.

'Not as good as the fountain but it will do,' she says and water runs down my face and my clothes suck my skin.

I say, 'It feels like not needing to be right.'

She says I should write that down but I do not need to.

'We will go broom shopping one day,' she says. 'You just wait.'

A trail of wet footprints dries on the subway platform. The train grinds its ax through the station, and I tingle at the thought of someone unseen pushing me onto the tracks. It whips past and the breeze tugs at our clothes. On the train she tells me how much she loves Christmas and I tell her how much I hate it but I never tell her or myself the truth about why and she snaps at me for the first time: 'Fuck it then.'

I walk to the other end of the train and count every clacking rail, every dinging doorbell, every rattling cup of change. Too much everything, and owed apologies. She can talk and talk and I will listen mostly and I will kiss her so so soft to shut her up, whisper in her ears, but maybe I just want to fuck. Maybe that is a lie, maybe. A sound that sounds like this. There is nothing in here, not like she thinks, nothing for long to want, and I want to give her all of it.

I step off the train before my stop and she follows. She catches up and takes my hand and we walk along the edge of the park and watch the lightning bugs flash. She calls them fireflies.

'Aimlessly walking around the city is the only time I don't feel completely crazy,' she says, and I laugh and she says she cannot tell if that laugh is 'with' or 'at.'

A man steps out from behind a tree and into the light and says hello. He is dirty and points down and pulls up the leg of his shorts and I think he is going to flash his dick but he sticks his finger into a crusty, bloody gash on his leg. I keep my eyes on his eyes and she walks faster and covers her mouth with her hand and I try to slow her down as we pass him.

'People usually give me money when I do that,' he says.

His eyes are resin, his teeth are tusks. I give him a look I hope seems like anger rather than fear and we walk away and he yells: 'Oh, such a tough guy!' I hear footsteps but try to keep our pace the same. He yells something else, I do not know what, and she squeezes my hand as hard as she can until I do not hear footsteps anymore and I glance over my shoulder and he is sitting on a bench, knifing his head with his fingers.

We turn a corner and run to the door of my building, out of breath. I fumble with my keys and we run up the stairs and as soon as the lock clicks in the apartment, we throw our clothes all over the place, jeans crumpled in a blossom again, and I fuck her and she fucks me and we fuck. She says she wants to build a sheet fort and hides under the covers and her head pops out and she says she is thirsty. She walks to the fridge and pours a glass of water and pokes a magnet on the fridge that says I HEART PORN.

'Is that true?' she says.

'Hell yes,' I say.

'What kind?' She uses both hands to raise the glass to her lips.

'Orgies,' I say.

She swallows. 'I prefer gang bangs.'

'I bet.'

'Hey, other than porn, I'm actually very conservative,' she says.

I say, 'Yeah, right,' with my face.

She hands me the water and I drink the rest in one large gulp. She walks across the room and sits in the white leather chair, nothing but yellow panties on, and hugs her knees until she cries and it is possible that there has never been anything more beautiful. She cries until she stops crying.

There is no noise outside and I say, 'I walked through a park on my way to work, just said, fuck it, I'll be a little late. It was chilly and gray and a stuffed animal was stuck in a tree and the tiered fountain in the square was flowing, ringed in flowers, white and pink.'

She wipes her cheeks with the back of a hand and says, 'You really have to watch out for those bears,' and I wonder how she knew the stuffed animal was a bear. I walk to her. I kiss her on the bloody kiss under her skin. She sniffs and wipes her nose.

'I'm going to invent a new way to hug, and hug you in a way that nobody has ever been hugged,' I say. 'A hug to end hugs.'

'We'll see,' she says, staring at the floor, and I stare at her stare.

I lean in close and she says, 'Your eyelashes are so long. They're like spiders.'

I pull her panties off, lift her in the air and she wraps her legs around me. She smiles and wipes off the last of the trails from her cheeks. We kiss.

'It feels like,' she says and I put a hand over her mouth and run my fingers through her hair and across the back of her head and say: 'I brush my teeth just to call you.'

She looks like she might cry again and I do not want any more tears so I stick a finger in her ass. It slides right in, nice, and she does not even stiffen her back. Her face is a strong, blank dare. I set her down slowly, bend her over and she says, 'Do whatever you want,' and I slip the finger in again and she stiffens, clamps down and I count silently in and out until she says, 'Stop.'

She turns and her eyes are pools and I look for myself in the curved reflections and she says the meanest thing she has ever said to me: 'I don't like you any more.'

I tell her that is the meanest thing she has ever said to me and this is my chance to move but I do not. She bites her lip and hugs me and takes it back, tries to. I sniff my finger and it is so clean that she must shit bleach.

'What does it feel like?' I say.

'Not pleasant,' she says, pulling up her panties.

'No, not that,' I say. "It."

She sighs.

'What was that sigh for?' I say and she says, 'Just pushing out feelings I don't want to deal with.'

I walk around the room backwards, one step behind the next, and she asks what I am doing and I tell her that you cannot know where you are going if you do not know where you've been and this gives me a better view of that.

'I want to see everything except what is right in front of me,' I say.

She sits in the white leather chair, hugs her legs again and presses her lips against her knees.

'It feels like knowing you are dreaming during a dream,' she says, 'and taking full advantage of all your sleep powers.'

A horn blast outside startles her and she laughs. I pick up a dirty shirt from the coffee table and throw it on the couch because somehow that seems better. She slides back in bed, rubs her stomach and stretches and her ribs are wonders and she says, 'All this is making me hungry.'

Blue flames crown a burner, oil pops and an egg sizzles. I count the pops and I count them, count, and carry the egg to her on the spatula.

'What are you doing with that?' she says.

'We're going to eat it,' I say. 'It might be too hot for you right now, though.'

'I can handle it,' she says. 'Do it.'

I flip it over on her stomach and she bolts up and shrieks. 'Oh! Oh! Oh! It's too hot!'

I scoop it off and blow on her stomach until she and the egg are cooler. Somehow the yolk does not break.

'Too bad it's not poached,' she says. 'Hey, I have something to tell you. Remember my wish? Well, I lied.'

I slide the egg between her breasts and pick at the whites with a fork.

'Needs salt and pepper,' I say. I hold the grinders up like trophies and grind both on her. 'Don't sneeze.' I stab the yolk with the fork and drag the golden ooze down to her navel with some swerves.

'Modern art,' she says.

'So what did you wish for?' I say.

I hold out a bite for her.

'Well, what are the wish rules?' she says. 'If I tell you, it might not come true.'

I feed her another salty and peppery bite. She asks how long this kind of treatment lasts and I say, 'Until you stop appreciating it.'

'Good answer,' she says. 'I guess that's the way it is with everything.'

Back and forth with the bites and I drag yolk over her nipples with the fork and lick it off.

'It's like we're living inside of a poem,' she says.

I feed her the last bite.

'Look, I know you're not going to say it back, and I know there is a lot of responsibility with these words but –' she stops and stares at me, waiting for a sign that it is okay to say them and I say, 'Look, there are so many better ways to say that, and saying it will take the place of them all.'

'Whatever, whatever,' she says. She gives me her 'Yeah, right' face and bites the insides of her lips. I count passing cars, many of them.

'Can you slap me or something?' she says.

She walks back to the white leather chair and perches in it, a cheek resting on her knees. Her panties match the yolk streaked across her skin.

'You sitting there is the second most beautiful thing I have ever seen,' I say.

'Second?' she says, lifting her head and raising her eyebrows.

'Yeah,' I say, 'second.'

'Well, what the hell is more beautiful than this?' She waves an arm across her body like a game-show girl displaying the grand prize, and says, 'Nothing,' and she is right but I say, 'I threw away a plastic bottle this morning when I was leaving the dangerous bear park. If not for that, you'd be number one. Easily.'

'Wait,' she says. 'You are talking about garbage right now, you fucking dick. You realize that?'

'Well, what happened when I threw that bottle away really blew my mind,' I say.

'I don't want to hear about it.' She swivels in the chair and looks out the window, and I look out, too, at the neck-bound baby dolls. I wrap my arms around her, press my neck against hers, and whisper: 'I was walking through the park.' I rub small circles into her bruise, as water-ripple-soft as fingers can be, and I count the circles.

'There was a breeze that rolled in and out like a soft wave at the boardwalk.' I run my fingers into her hair and she closes her eyes, her lashes lovely.

'I took the last sip of my drink and saw a trash can.' I kiss the ring of teeth marks.

'The breeze picked up right as I tossed the bottle toward the trash can and it hit the rim and I thought, 'How could I have just missed that?' and I was mad but the bottle shot straight across to the other side, hit the rim again and bounced high into the air in a long, slow arc and froze at the top, like somebody was trying to tell me something important, and I couldn't figure out what it was but it was beautiful in its holding still, and it fell straight in.'

She spins in the white leather chair and looks at me – this is where I am – and I say it again, slower, softer, holding still, not fading but seeing her in her eyes, every color burning into black holes.

'It hit the rim ...' I draw its path in the air with a finger, slowly, '... shot straight across ... hit the other rim ... floated ... froze ... fell in.'

She says, 'I know you are just going to steal me for your stories.'

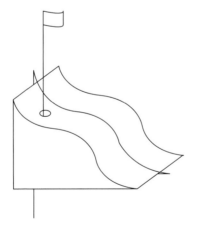

AME
MUS

I C A N A R D

ROSIE ŠNAJDR

Eight-thousand eels per annum for the quarry. The Barnack rag was egg stone. Oolitic. Lime. From sand that tickled gills of fish came this great bed.

Shells tugged in the lub dub of the lake. Growing great coats of calcite precipitate, the dead joining hand to hand with the dead. Twelve month apprenticed to

M a s t -
e   r
Mason
P e a -
r c e ,
should have been about learning to plug feathers and sheer straight the rock. 'Of an Eagle you were

Aart was an imperfect study. The sculpture School sang to him and, despite his surren-der to the higher calling, he would shirk. The large stone clept, Aart, willn't you then look?' 'Maybe I shalln't.' The sawyers spat. The sawyers tapped a line of pins and stones sheered off in neat blocks.

men exasperated to see him squat with stick to pattern in the mud, when he

The sawyers praised the Virgin. The old wet sleds slopped over by the Welland are bound for the Fens. Where there is passage to permit it,

hulking beasts sweat and snort against taught sheets. Where there is not, pole-men swear and sing in pretence of leisure

b u t
t h e y
too do
sweat.
A l l
winter. Bede the Banker worked the stones to the Master Mason's map. Here'n's the top stone of the pillar of n'arch, there'n's the key.

It was, in fact, the second key, since the boy had been given the simplest job

of neatening up an edge and had lopped out the corner with a clum-sy thunk. The chile was more'n interested in the hansdome triple-arrow mark that ended work on every block, which meant only money-owed to Bede. He would maybe make a Carver, if he pressed his luck.

The Carver Masons were a heathen bunch. Lex had been overheard bragging the Virgin in his relief had the face of his whore and went unpaid for that work. He had a mind, he said, to sell it, with tighter lips, to a vil-lage church. In cups that night he had tried to spirit his work away from the site on the back of a mule.

She Who Shows the Way Cause of Our Joy Rose of Sharon Rose without Thorns Throne of Wisdom Bundle of Myrrh Lily of the Field Ark of the Covenant Morning Star Star of the Sea Untier of Knots Tower of David Gate of Heaven Panaghia Most Holy Queen of Heaven Queen of Sinners Donna Del Cielo Queen of the Angels Queen of Peace God-Bearer Deipara Meter Theou Blessed Mother Pity Mother of Good Counsel Mother of God Mercy Mother of Victory Loving Mother Holy Virgin of Virgins Most Pure Ever-Virgin Parthenos Blessed Virgin Mary Mediatrix Interlocutor Queen of Matyrs Queen of Confessors Mama Queen of Fami

The tree branch
lies   he'd made
L a d y   his lever
Queen of   s n a -
Patriarchs   p p -
Our Lady of
Caysasay   Our   on a path
Lady of Ta' Pinu   through
Our   Lady   of   the ra-
Salambao   Our   v'nous
Lady of the Im-   F e n .
maculate Concept-
ion Our Lady of the
Gate of Dawn in
Vilnius Our Lady
of Guidance Our
Lady of Sorrows
Mother Our Lady
of Grace Our Lady
of Chartres Our
Lady of Charity
Our Lady of Leb-
anon Our Lady of
Loreto Our Lady of
Light Our Lady of
Ransom Our Lady
Nursing Lapis La-
zuli Spouse of the
Holy Spirit Nuestra
Señora New Eve
The Good Woman
Full of Grace Beat-
issima Holy Mary
K e c h a r i t o m e n e
Hagia Maria Sancta
Maria Comfort of
the Afflicted Health
of the Sick Refuge
of Sinners Mary
Help of Christians
Cause of Our Sal-
vation Causa Salutis

ed, as well it might,
and the scul-pture
came down in the
spirit of rock and
split the beast like

The thief was left to the bog, a
body to join the bog bodies of
yore. The Bankers said it must
be justice. When news reached
them, the Sawyers praised

His fingers applied to the
raggedy edge of the brok-
en branch and he halloed.
Hallo-ha. 'What's not been
known about stone here,

a bladder-sack. The stone and
the animal not being his, he
fled. He was found, yellow
bloated wreck, wrong-footed
for all his local knowledge
t h e V i r g i n .
T h e   w h o r e
went less well
f e d . F i r m a n
was a Fixer.

by Lex the lightfoot,
is that it's heavy. As
much, it's good the
Carvers don't have
charge to pick 'em up.'

H a l l o o - h a - h a .
Unfortunate already
in sons, he was not re-
minded of his words,
when a lewisson slipt

**Constellated galaxies of
violent yellow exploded
into the ether. The thin poly-
propylene bottle crushed
in the pincer of his fingers**

and his **emitted a terrified fart, but** s t o n e . T h e
o w n **it was already too late. The** C a r v e r s ,
F e l i x **mustard had landed. He** w h o m h e
caught **pushed back his chair and** scorned last,
t h e **stood up, his arms splayed** bore blank,

in a posture of surrender, irresponsible faces but
his throat clicking inchoate- joked about St Peter's
ly. The men beside him were Keys. The Bankers,
startled upright, fearing his whom he had also
croaking symptomatic of scorned, chipped on
blockage. Was there some over stern whispers.

bolus   of The Sawyers, whom he always knowing
barbeque scorned, praised the Virgin Mary. not the-
l o d g e d The farmers, fishers, thatchers, s e c r e t s
in   the and peat-cutters, they all looked of geo-
entrance upon the building-as a magic, m e t r y .
to   his
windpipe?

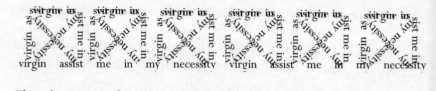

virgin assist me in my necessity virgin assist me in my necessity

The white magic of geometry was maculate. As penance for his winter crimes

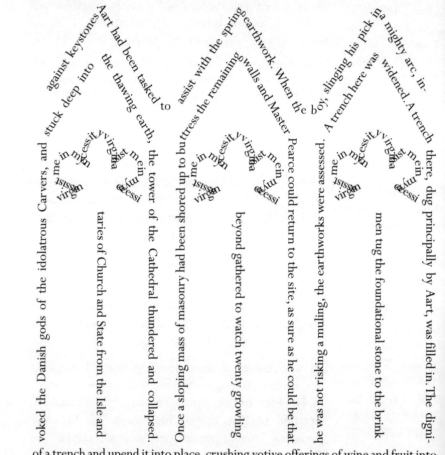

Aart had been tasked to assist with the spring earthwork. When the boy, slinging his pick in a mighty arc, in-voked the Danish gods of the idolatrous Carvers, and against keystones stuck deep into the thawing earth, the tower of the Cathedral thundered and collapsed. Once a sloping mass of masonry had been shored up to buttress the remaining walls and Master Pearce could return to the site, as sure as he could be that he was not risking a muling, the earthworks were assessed. A trench here was widened. A trench there, dug principally by Aart, was filled in. The digni-taries of Church and State from the Isle and beyond gathered to watch twenty growling men tug the foundational stone to the brink

of a trench and upend it into place, crushing votive offerings of wine and fruit into the mud. A Churchman, robes undulating in the wind, his hem scuffed with mud

and donkey shit, tapped the top of the stone and said a prayer. Then work went on.

A
wrig-
gle for the
sniggler Sargasso
snakes undulate at slime-
weight slopping into sopping
sloughs of fishskin snakes coil
and feint in suppurating
shanks of slakewater
baitpot sheen of
roil to copulate
to mate of
supping
slur-
p-

A well-intentioned man to the right wrapped his arms quite uselessly around the choking man's waist and began to squeeze for his life. Men further down the table, who had risen in expectation of an impromptu speech, looked at their brogues to avoid the shocking spectacle of the embrace. Only the men opposite had grasped the true horror of the situation. The women hadn't shaken the condiments! The wives had bought cheap yellow mustard; mustard with

too much water. The factory-workers, unguilded and unmannerly, had overlooked a faulty nozzle. His sacred apron was quite, quite ruined. Ern surveyed the map of occupied territory on his lambskin, full sheepish. He knew it had been cramp in his hand. He had taken three through the first degree before lunch and the handle of his paddle was unpadded. The whole experience had been punishing. May I ask the brethren how to clean a lambskin apron? How to remove the stain from that which I must be buried in? The stain?

p -
ery
mouthed
suckers
air-shunning
sheckles of speckle
light sheening suck suck
eye-popping most blue lidless surprise snapping sinew side of fish-shank sunk
in the oil of fish-bodies
scum raking the
watersurface
an orgy
of cur-

The stain is immortal. You cannot separate the mortal sin from the grave matter. You can't repent American mustard, Ern.

li-
cues
for-
nicating
ring-0-ring
twine gyre whorl

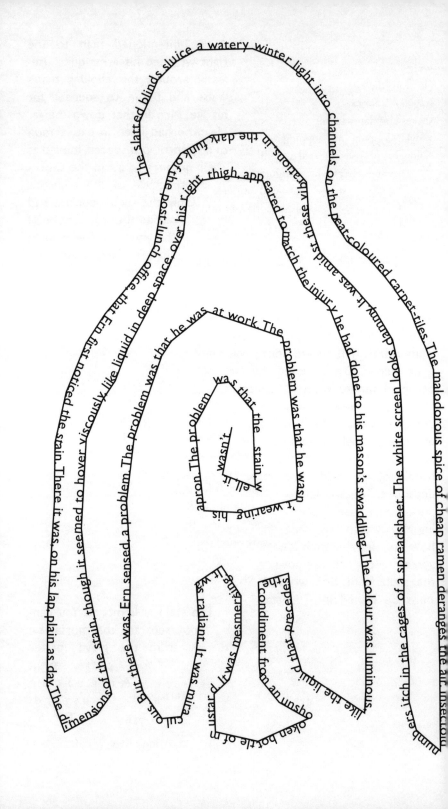

The slatted blinds sluice a watery winter light into channels on the peat-coloured carpet-tiles. The malodorous spice of cheap ramen deranges the air. Insect cloud numbers itch in the cages of a spreadsheet. The white screen looms damply. It was amid these vibrations in the dark junk of the post-lunch office that Ern first noticed the stain. There it was, on his lap, plain as day. The dimensions of the stain though it seemed to hover viscously like liquid in deep space over his right thigh appeared to match the injury he had done to his mason's swaddling. The colour was luminous like the liquid that preceded the condiment from an unshoken bottle of mustard. It was radiant. It was miraculous. But there was. Ern sensed a problem. The problem was that he was at work. The problem was that he wasn't wearing his apron. The problem was that the stain well it wasn't.

actually there, in any real sense.

As real as it wasn't, it was becoming clear that the stain was not, identical to the one that no amount of saddle-soap had been able to shift from his lambskin vestment. It was, in fact, a new shape of stain. This was a stain that had eyes. From this stain emerged a nose. Here the underneath of a lip. At the top, the hint of a diadem. This stain was a vision of the

'Holy Mother of God!'

That's right Ern, that's right.

An almighty crack, like thunder struck, sends Ern skittling back from his desk in his wheeled office chair; his frightened hands spidering, as though about to strike a complex chord on a organ. The visitation on his corduroy vanishes like holy water down a plug-hole. As he watches it vanish, the thunderclap becomes the tap, tap, tap it had always been and, with mouth agog, Ern stares up at the figure looming in the hallway. It is not death. It's not the Ghost of Christmas past. It's Steve. Steve opens the door.

'Aloha, buddy.' Steve pauses to accustom himself to the gloom.

'Jeeze, you look something awful Ern. Are you sick buddy?'

'I'm not sick, buddy. You startled me is all.'

'Well I sure am sorry about that Ern.' Steve eyeballs him, as if unconvinced.

The masons look at each other. The mason who is standing twiddles his pinkie ring in the awkward silence. The masons look at each other.

'Did you come for any particular reason Steve?'

'Oh, yes, Ern. Master Mason requested your presence at the Lodge this weekend. You see, he's worried that he hasn't seen you at all this month. He's worried you took the, ah, mustard predicament to heart. We're all worried about you, buddy.'

The ring girdled the corpulent index finger, the flesh coming up around it pert and red. Among the rank and file brothers, the done thing was to shift the signet down the hand as the years passed. The ring hooked on the adolescent index, loose as a promise. Years of surfeit of surplus left it straining on a buxom pinkie. This custom brooked stealth. Business could be done with staunch rejectionists. Mistresses could meet their men naked; blushing and unbribable. He was locked in. Ern wasn't wearing his a[...] Pierce. He was wedded to the brotherhood. It wasn't like that for

The company in the Guildhall shewed the difference: dust in the ears of the working men, their hands nocke[d] with scars, still trembling from the ring of the hammer; the mercantile pomp of the new lot. The soiled leather aprons of the working men were heavy, sweat-soaked. It was a mercy to get out of them at down of sun. The humps of them hillo--cking the dust floor of the site. The new ones had adopted the apron, stiff and clean, as symbols of their solidarity. They wore them all night. 'Brothers.' They weren't. 'Brothers, we are gathered here today to show hands.' Aart's were the hands of a barber surgeon: raw-boned an[d] drawn-out. They manifested the precision he had shown since finding his place amongst the junior carvers. Aart had come t[o] fit the chink in labour at the Chapel left by the body rotting in the bog. A working man's silece filled the hall.

The hourglass finger, purpling and putrefact, tap, tap, tapped on the printout. "All's I'[m] saying is: 'It doesn't add up Ern, it doesn't add up.'" It did add up. About the only thing it d[id] There are two proposed for membership of the Guild today. Aart Corpus and Edit Hereward.' Applause. 'Those of you on the Ely build,' Pearce intoned, 'will know well our eagle-eyed son Aart.

do was that. What it didn't do was fig leaf the last fiddle. It was a firearm, smoki[ng] gently, between double-entries. "I don't understand it, Ern. You're our numbers man for; what, twelve years?" Ern makes what is either a short slow nod, or he hangs his head. "Well, I don't pretend to know how you do it. I'm not a number man. But you always did it, only, this time, you haven't. And it's real serious. The I[...]

are into us. They sent proceedings. Ern, I'm sorry, you're toast." Ern remembers toast.

The novelty bread-stamp that had impressed the image of the virgin onto his morning

They will know his fledgling clodding.' 'He ruined mine keystone n'arch, that chick.' Laughter brings a bright blush to the aquiline face of the youth whose beard is not quite through. 'They will know too that his

the image would appear anyway, when he didn't use it.

'Ern.' He studies the older man's face in silence. Out come the teeth.

slice of wholewheat. The way

I'm not taking this for the team, Pierce.' He studies the placid flesh.

A range of possible expressions shuffle beneath the ... Even your shrink is worried about you.

A smile. 'Ern, you've been having a time lately. Think about what you're

You're not in your right mind. You've been hallucinating.

work has come to scratch the perfection of the senior carving brethren. You may have been lucky enough to see his first Madonna and not have know it. Which is to say, she lives. She. Lives.'

'And here's Edit Hereward.' A man steps forward. 'Son of the parish. Man of ideas. Provider of plenty. Not. Not, I might add, as though it were not obvious, a stonemason by trade. 'Here, he own'n my fief, doth he not?' Laughter. The man lowers his jaw and begins to speak saying.

It doesn't make any sense.' Ern thought of the Virgin that appeared in his mirror at night. Ern thought of the Lady impressed upon his pillow in the morning. He thought about the figure of the Holy Mother in the worn rubber of his tire tread. The kind brown eyes, imploring him to conscience, in his rear view. Now he feels her flesh hanging from his very bones. There is a key twisting in the oaken doors of the lodge and all within't will answer to fate. All within't are locked in. He screws off his ring. He looks at him level. 'I'm tipping the tables in the temple, Pierce.'

an open-mouthed speech. "If I may speak for myself, Master Mason?" Just Pearce just nods. "Am I a stonemason? No. Wherefore then do I find myself before you all? Quite. Well have I seen the

Chapel rising from the earth beside the Cathedral at Ely. It was a magic to me. Yes. It was a great magic. I am a man with great interest in balances. I am a man with interest in your craft. I want to learn about your magic. I want to be taught.'

A flat blackened toe worms through a hole in a dusty workman's shoe and draws a pentagram through the dust and straw, causing a rising commotion of sniggers to burst forth

The Ancrene Wiss, a brother for his sistern writ, 'read daily my words, when your prayers be done?' His a freeman's manual for confinement. A paperwork to contain the lives of Anchoresses. Praise be to Mother Mary, I wouldn't have managed my life in a box without it. Outer Rule: Welcome to the office of the dead. The Anchorite in Anchorhold is subject to a burial rite. Timor mortis conturbat me. A bishop said that, then a mason did up the final brick. Asceticism against the five senses, my brother writ, on paper stained with animal fat. By my troth, sistern, thou cannot be trusted to be looked at. Hate your window. Lash up thy curtain tight. Do not be seen by men, whose darting eyes will spoil you in God's sight. Hagioscope—squint: a window for Mass. Ichor or liquor and singing of lambs. A casement for other-wordly needs, the passing of porridge and piss. A window for advising the villagers, curtained off with sack. Performing the Ancrene Riwle in the mornings and the Little Office of Our Lady in the afternoons. Outside are temptations, tortures, torrents, terrors. The fragile womanish vessel, a tender morsel among the canaille. Sister, you cannot not be enwombed by bricks and freedom find. Iwis. He tells me how to prey and how to contribute to the church prayers. He tells me which foot to wash first. Inner Rule: Reject the label Anchoress. What need be there for gendering this calling thus, ywiss women outstrip men four to two? Call me 'pelicano solitudinis' if you must but never call me 'Miss.' I am gaining heaven. I am private with God. I am requited in Christ. The outer rule governs diet, work, feast days, clothing, visitation, servants, and related mundane aspects of anchoritic life. The outer rule governs moral practices not enjoined by vow.

Daryl Scroggins

Net Sales

He was not proud of the work he did selling franchises for a business that had no real product line. But he didn't see himself as much different from the people he was pitching to, so if they bought in they just didn't come in where he had and that was where they went wrong.

His wife wouldn't look at him unless something good had happened. This was useful to remember when he came in from his after-work liquor store run and didn't want her to notice the size of the grocery sack he held.

She was reading.

'You still reading?' he asked.

'My ear is killing me,' she said.

He moved quickly from the front door to the kitchen, but he could feel that she had glimpsed him between entry and walls. 'I saw someone from work at the liquor store,' he said from the kitchen. A story always helped in navigating dead zones and hazardous areas. 'Guy named Landers. He stepped right up to me and accused me of costing him the monthly productivity award.'

She turned to face the hall that was aiming at her and he pulled his head back.

'I took him over to the tequila samples. It's Thursdays when they set the table up, and that woman who always looks like she's ironing hands out the pill-cup shots.'

'Why'd he say that,' she asked, turning a page.

'He suggested I had suggested that he divert some of his revenue stream to expenses and claim them later, if that would allow him to sustain the run he had going. Then the man started crying. Just leaking a little, really. He told me his tires were so bald the cords were showing.'

'So you told him to steal from the company,' she said, still in lower case.

'Of course I didn't. I told him that a managed bifurcation of revenue streams was often a useful tactic for prolonging sales momentum, so long as reporting requirements are anticipated and responses have been readied.'

'Ha. And then?'

'We sampled all three of each of everything. He could see that the ironing lady wouldn't have been so generous if I hadn't been there. And then I gave him some free tips. I told him it's what you come up with after you run through everybody you know that counts. You need to show how much you care like it's true.'

'What did he say to that?'

Stirring a pitcher he realized he was out of storyline. He tilted his head and looked down the hallway. Her thumb slipped and the right side of her pages took a breath. 'How's your ear?' he said, and he brought in the tray with the pitcher and glasses.

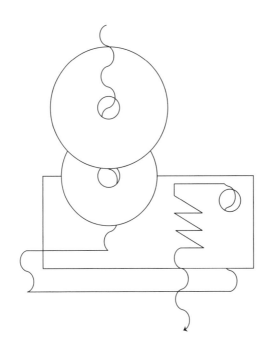

Julie Reverb

Trapeze

Some of us are born understudies, waiters in the wings, wobblers on orbits far from the spotlight.

It's fine day-to-day; in the office kitchen; at the school prom. But it's not fine on the trapeze – which is where I was.

We were a small outfit (two boys, three girls), decked up as playing cards to soar over corporate events. I stood in for anyone too sore to perform. More often, I was asked to drive us to conference centres, the muffler dragging on the freeway.

It was a shit business, and I had dropped out of school to be in it. I'd send my parents kitsch cards with lies on the back: famous fans, standing ovations.

Hanging on for the big time would never work. Something had to change – and sometimes something needs a push.

It was a team-building day for software geeks whose eyes lazered on our high-rise leotards. We joked about their creased faces while setting up above them.

Simon – an old ballet dancer – called in hungover. I was reeled in to cover.

I know I started strong, in full-bodied swing. I counted bald-spots and saw how the buffet looked tastier upside down. Sal – the queen in the royal flush – looked fantastic as usual, if slightly tired.

No, I don't remember pushing her. There's no footage. On the trapeze, everyone knows their place. All I know is she wasn't in hers.

Stephen Mortland

Two Fictions

EGGS

We boys are busy boiling eggs on stovetops. Watch
the surface of the water: wait for it to snap and bubble.
Wait for the water to toss the eggs against the saucepan
wall. Two boys stop me on the bleacher stairs. The
one that talks has a face like a guppy, lips that puck-
er, cheeks that plateau. He scratches his head. Spectral
white freckles appear all along his collar.

The other boy watches. Grapes for eyes, eager to be
surprised. My ears are popping, filled with the sound
of eggs clinking against steel as the water cooks them
inside out.

'Well, are you?' he asks me. The word *virgin* sounds
funny leaving his mouth. Sounds like he's been holding it in his cheeks, plumping it up with saliva before
spitting it out onto the concrete.

I can't cool the eggs. I run the shells under cold
water, but the flesh in the middle is burning. I hold
an egg with my fingertips and thwack it against the
countertop. It doesn't shatter so much as buckle, like
I punched the egg in its belly. From the cratered dim-
ple, spider legs spread across its bald head. I wedge my
thumb under the puckering shell. The two boys are
watching me silently. Starving. They each want to eat
another boy, but they don't want to eat one another.
Maybe they're in love. They don't love me, which is
why they ask me if I'm a virgin. God is a virgin, I say
to myself. God loves virgins – like Mary – who is a

virgin and also a woman. Virgins are gods and virgins are women, and I am neither of those things.

The membrane wrinkles and folds as it gasps from under the shell. I have eggshell under my thumbnail and small eggshell particulates stuck to my skin. The husk is coming off in large tinfoil pieces, and the egg beneath it is wet. I answer quickly, then shove the entire egg into my mouth so that I can't say anything else. I run up the remaining stairs. I can't speak, can't breathe, but I can hear them beneath me laughing, and I know that they are really in love.

PILLS

It was too much for him on his own. Counting out the pills, forcing the pills to the back of his tongue, coaxing them down his throat. But he could, at least, open his mouth for me.

The age taking hold of his face and frame didn't frustrate him. He had vacated his body entirely. The house was full of thieves, he told me.

It was early evening. He sat in the blue and yellow folding chair above the steps. His cheek bloomed, and the skin of his lip was peppered with stray tobacco fragments. His naked stomach, mottled and bloated, rested on his lap.

'A fly's been trapped in my house for a week,' he told me. 'I can't get hands on it, and it's grown so fat off all my food that I can hear it no matter what room I'm in.'

'It looks like it might rain,' I said, taking him by the hands and pulling him from the chair. I set my palm on the lower half of his back to guide him. His skin was damp and gave way when I pushed. He felt like a hollow, rubber baby doll.

Two of the three lightbulbs had burnt out. The kitchen smelled faintly of talcum and bleach. I fumbled with the bottle until its top popped off. We sat down and I counted the pills in my cupped palm. He told me not to count them, to let them puddle until my palm was full.

'I want you to hold me after I swallow them,' he said. 'Can you do that?'

His lips were chapped. When they touched my palm, his lips felt like scabs. I held the glass up to his mouth. Water leaked and dribbled down his chin, leaving a shadow on the knee of my pants. He stuck out his tongue, wiggled it like a child, proving to me that his cheeks were empty. I could hear the fly buzzing above us, looking everywhere for a way out.

Kate Wyer

Two Fictions

BRIDGETON, NEW JERSEY

Get me a banana Laffy-Taffy, says the woman next to the dumpster. She holds out the nickel in the palm of her left hand. Her right is busy drawing circles of hot pink lipstick onto the apples of her cheeks. I take the nickel. The woman uses both hands to rub the pigment into her skin.

The penny candy is on the bottom shelf, near the door. All the dust and exhaust fumes blow over it, coating the wax paper wrappers with a film of South Jersey.

Using a single finger, I push the flavors around until I find the banana near the bottom. It is hard and stale.

The counter girl presses the buttons on her register. A pack of Marlboro lights, with the receipt of purchase taped around them, sticks out from her apron. Her forearm is coated in something shiny and wrapped in clear plastic, to protect the new tattoo of a name, the same one as on her name badge.

Six cents, she says. She barely sees me, her focus is outside, by the far dumpster.

I put the nickel on the counter and take a penny from the dish.

This isn't for that lady, is it? She asks, her hip leaning into the counter.

I shake my head no, then take the key with the soup ladle attached to it.

The bathroom is on the far side of the building. There is long-haul trucker piss everywhere, everywhere except the place I've stashed my acorns.

I lift the porcelain lid of the toilet's water tank. The bag of acorns is suspended in the water reserve, the nut's bitter tannins flushed with each push of the lever as man after man relieves himself. Clean potable water filling and draining. The water in the tank is clear, instead of tea-brown, which tells me the acorns are ready to come out.

I had already tested them for worms by dumping them into the tank and seeing which floated. After discarding two handfuls of them, the rest were solid and edible.

A man's fist pounds the door.

Come'on, he says.

I grab the roll of coarse paper towels, and wrap some around the dripping bag. I replace the tank's lid and then undo the door's lock.

The man backs up a little when he sees me, then smirks and tries to lean into my body as it passes.

Water continues to drain from the bag as I walk across the lot, mindful of the counter girl's eyes. If she sees me hand over the candy, I'll most likely be banned from the store too. I see her pouring coffee grounds into fresh filters, her shoulders telling me her mind is absorbed in her task.

Psst, I hiss under my breath.

The woman lifts a hand above the drainage pipe. I walk to her and then slide down the slight bank to join her out of the wind.

She takes the candy from my hand.

You'll pull your teeth right out, I say.

She shrugs as her eyes try to focus on my face.

A SILENCE

Mom lined up us on the linoleum floor of the kitchen. She sloshed water over and around and under our bodies. Plain washcloths were on our foreheads. I remember us there, all nine. Naked, sweating, talking in tongues. Rooted to the floor by visions. I remember when the sound cut out, when the pain in my head imploded and there was nothing.

And then the white nothing of the hospital. I opened my swollen eyes and saw a TV. On the TV, a cartoon dog moved his mouth. I did not at first notice the silence. *I am not home*, I thought. Three of my siblings were also in the room. They were sitting up and drinking juice from small cups and tiny straws. They were focused on the dog. A cat entered the frame and the dog chased it around and around a tree. My siblings laughed. I saw their faces move and their bodies rock backwards. I began to laugh too, to join them.

Imagine yourself, eight, laughing at a cartoon dog chasing a cartoon cat. And then imagine three siblings turning at once in horror at the sound you've made. *A laugh*, you think. I laughed. It was funny. The dog and the tree and all that. But their faces. You knew from their faces that something about you had changed.

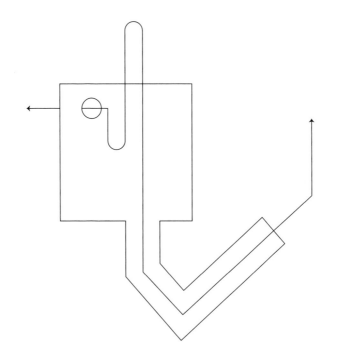

Gordon Lish

Two Fictions

PETARD

You'd come into a room.

No, go into it.

Or is it in to it?

It could be it's in to it and not into it. Also go. Not come but go. Isn't that what they taught you – go for away from yourself, come for to you? Well, I'm sorry, that's what they taught me, didn't they?

Oh, there's so much of it heaping up!

This is the reason why I stay inside. But do I have to tell you it is not always going to be in the cards for you to keep indoors? There are occasions, incidents, certain obligatoriums, things come up. Like yesterday, for instance. Don't ask me to remember why, but there were no two ways about it, I had to go out.

Oh, Jesus, Jesus, Jesus.

To Brooklyn.

May I tell you something?

Here is my personal opinion of Brooklyn.

Never again.

Am I making myself clear to you?

I'm sure it's a very swell borough and I am sure that there are plenty of ultra swell people there who have to live in it, but to tell you the bitter truth, Brooklyn is not for me. Ditto, forgive me, the Bronx. You want to hear chapter and verse as to the reasons I (Gordon!) have no use for Brooklyn, to begin with, including, while we're at it, Walt Whitman?

Pay attention.

People there are given to saying they when they are standing there mentioning to you one human being, reference-wise, okay?

Or them when the situation in their mind fits the case.

People there say kind of and sort of when you do not have to say anything but the thing you want to say.

I'm serious.

I already told you – this was just yesterday.

Here's a for instance for you as to a selection from yesterday's experience.

'I really and truly sort of love living here.'

Here's one for kind of.

'The mayor of the five boroughes, he's kind of a really pretty great dude, don't you agree?'

If somebody says kind of and sort of or sort of or kind of, I don't have to think twice to tell you almost everything else there is to be said about them.

Oh-oh, you caught that or didn't you?

Level with me.

How long have I got?

Got hoisted on my own whatever.

Steady, pal.

You think it wasn't a trap I laid for you?

All right, relax.

I mean well, you know?

You fell for it or into it, unless it's in to.

People.

People in Brooklyn can't wait for them to tell you something's multiple.

Here's another for instance.

It's a direct statement, quotation, not, if you don't mind, quote.

Anyway, here it is.

The statement.

'Oh, I have multiple opinions regarding the mayor's plan for making empty soda cans edible.'

Here's another for instance, a simpler one, a touch, but not much, less political.

'Oh, I have multiple friends with residences on that block who got pulled in for questioning trying to vote for Bernie multiple times.'

You live where I live and you go along with the spirit of your intelligence and you accordingly stay indoors where the civilized belong, you don't hear nobody saying to you multiple this and multiple that multiple times.

But I could be rong.

Yet when have I been rong?

Just for the record, here's a further example.

'Oh, I gave *Leaves of Grass* multiple readings. Loved it, loved it, loved it!'

Those were citations of multiple examples.

Hang on. I want to add something. We're not going on to the next thing yet until I have added something. You hear what I'm saying? I want to add something first. It's that, not the fact that, there's nobody in Brooklyn old enough to know what Bill Clinton's middle name is, or that he sat there and under oath testified to a grand jury that he didn't do it. That's what?

Is it perjury or just mendacity while sworn to tell the truth? Do the selfsame multiplicities know POTUS then got himself a spot on prime time for him to swear to the nation he didn't do it? You hear me? Swear. With his whole face, not to mention the hair, swear. Oh, but in the course of when the man did do it, or was doing it, tell me what degree of the citizenry of Brooklyn have been made aware of the president's reaching out (oh, God, 'reaching out'!) and taking to hand a cigar and – well, I'm sorry, I was tutored too thoroughly in the finesses of speech for me to tell you what it later came out it occurred to the showrunner to do with it.

I know all about reaching out.

I know all about out-there.

I know all about Stormy Daniels.

Do you know all about Monica Lewinsky?

It is my understanding that during the episodes of her friendship with the president of the United States of America, she and William tarried over certain passages of *Leaves of Grass* multiple times.

A tois.

This is a Brooklynish thing.

My question to you is this.

No, not to, never to you, but, fuck, for you, for!

When they were sort of doing it, was the cigar in there already or did he fit it in there in a kind of flourish afterwards?

Unless it's afterward.

Look, am I not willing to learn?

I'm old, old enough for me to hear in my memory when Brooklyn was officially on the books as Ozone, but I am nonetheless more than willing.

Viz. to learn.

The answer is Jefferson.

The fellow went from Arkansas to Yale to Oxford to you-know-where.

That's where he was when he was introduced to, or introduced himself to, Miss Lewinsky.

Hey, when I say introduce, am I just whistling Dixie or practicing deep exegesis?

Reaching out – oh, man, may the saints preserve us!

Donald J. Trump went from one of the outer boroughs to rack and ruin.

Unless it's wrack.

I'm willing to stand corrected if it's wrack.

Here's a question for you – are there different qualities of bullshit or aren't they all at bottom bullshit?

Are there grades thereof?

Here's another brain-teaser – say you have the same and the same and the same, how many differences do you already have?

Oh yeah, sure, sure, multiple ones, I get it, I get it – please, you're making me sick – quit it, willya, okay?

Pay attention – I, Gordon J. Lish, found Brooklyn gahhhh.

Oh, here's another ponsay – I was well along in interaction engaging with a person everybody said was the smartest person in Brooklyn, so I says to this

person 'The ineradicable onton is coiled in tsmis afore-
thought, so what's your take on that, yes or no?'

You know what the person said?

The person said to me, 'Mr Lish, don't you mean
this?'

Here's something else a Brooklynite yesterday said
to me.

'How come is it it's William J. Clinton and it's
Donald J. Trump and it's Gordon J. Lish and why
don't you have the brains to get yourself the hell out
of here before dark?'

I wasn't stumped.

This is one of the lustrous reasons why I am going
to move heaven and earth to keep myself from ever
going back there ever again.

You want to know something?

I have already forgotten why I went there to
Brooklyn in the first place.

Here's a fresh ponsay for you – if you declare the
berserk application of the word multiple unbearable,
are you not, in virtue of the declaring, bearing it?

Listen, when I was a child and had no choice but
to go to Brooklyn every whipstitch for me to be kept
abreast of the unfolding perdition of my grandma and
grandpa, there'd be plenty of aunts and uncles there
in that building in Brooklyn, plus my own personal
Reggie and Phillie, all of whom, all of these people,
they would have all assembled themselves in a room
not far from the room where the expiring relations lay,
and what would be going on in the room that wasn't

the deathroom? They would all of them in there be in there sitting all around a big old-country table playing pinochle, okay?

So along comes I (Gordon!), and I (Gordon!) goes into the room, and before you know it, before you can say Jack Robinson, as the saying used to be enigmatically said back in the day, before the rubber's had itself an opportune minute for it to meet the road in, you're spotted.

Discerned.

The hazard of your presence has become known.

Lickety-split, the word goes, has gone, out.

It makes, has made, its way from one to the other of the card-players.

Aunts, uncles, all of the grown-ups, not to leave out of the line-up my own Regina (Reg) and (Phil) Philip.

Listen.

Pay attention.

It goes, it went, like this.

'Little pitchers have big ears.'

Did you hear that?

Were you really giving it your total like incorporation?

Right in the room not far from the room where Rachel Lish and where Isaac Lish were, uh, you know, sort of succumbing kind of, everyone, all of the aunts and all of the uncles, plus my own two personal forebears, unless it's forbears or forebearers or one or another evasive variant elaborated thereupon,

their having, these Lishes, unless it was really and truly Lishkowitzes and there was nobody in Brooklyn
who was kidding me when they would whisper to
me altogether entre nousishly in my ear Lish are you
kidding are you kidding are you out of your mind are
you so ghastrishly bereft of ferstandt, mmm? – whilst
one among them or whilst all of them, all, all, he or
they having come to know that you (Gordon!) were
crouching back behind a chair or were down on all
fours down under the table in famished pursuit of
every dropped petard of the garish cardroom candy
called in the day All Sorts. Honest, that's it, or it was
it, All Sorts – in the course of the card-playing, in the
course of their playing cards, not unlikely not pinochle but not improbably gin rummy or just plain rummy
or bridge or canasta or double canasta or casino or war,
the word went out.

Would go.

'Look alive, people – little pitchers have bigs ears.'

Alors, the errorfulness of it all.

It just keeps heaping up.

Hold it.

Heap and up?

Mmm.

Monsters!

You know what?

You want to know what?

It is all of it insupportable, that's what!

My God, Brooklyn's not even the half of it, is it?

I mean, what about the Bronx, Staten Island,
Queens!

If you want to know what takes the cake, that's what takes the cake – the illimitable insupportability of it all, the boroughs spelled boros and the bridges and tunnels with not anywhere among them a designation that any two taxi drivers ever agree on.

Mind me.

Oy gevalt, the contingencies! The consonants! The acoustics! The Jews!

Boys and girls, if I come across you saying agency, I am going to enter your name and its middle initial on a list I have been developing wherein all listed in it get killed, rrrr?

Here's another ponsay or the dwelling upon.

Back in the day when the day managed to merit one's being in it, the telephone operator said to you, when spelling to you, for surety's sake, what you'd said, the operator'd say arah.

Emes.

The operator would say to you, 'Is that gee-oh-ar-ah-dee-oh-en?'

Good God, when I started this, when I began it, set out to set all of this forth for you, I thought I was under the impression that I thought moderately highly of you, in, as it were, the plausible estimates of esteem.

As if we happily inhabited, one with the other, the habitable.

But I can tell you don't care about the candy I still care like crazy about.

Perhaps the word PROLEP – never mind.

Your topor notwithstanding, the thing of it is what the thing of it always is – chi parla, right?

You elevated the 'receiver' and expected that there be said: 'Number, please?' And it was, it was! My God, those were the days when you went in to or into a room wherein they (as in some many several more than one) were playing fan-tan or hearts or poker or crazy eights.

You enter, have entered, in Brooklyn, for unforgettable for instance, where there were Lishkowitzes dying in pairs.

You go in to or into the room where everybody's biding HIS time.

Maybe nobody in so many words said it. Maybe the statement arose from an utterance one heard in another jurisdiction instead. A permutation of a locution, all its components recollected rong.

You see that?

Tell the truth.

Were you on your toes at the top of your game?

I'm not.

But I'm in Manhattan, okay?

Call.

'Little pitchers have big ears.'

I mean, shitfire, what's the deal with that, in your personal opinion as a consumer of the forensic?

Plus what about the J's?

That's 212-348-6448.

But hurry before I have gone, or have come, unto HIM, mmm?

Unless it's un to.

PIECE

What am I if not an irridentist at heart! So authenti-
cally am I what I just claimed of myself, didn't I go to
the motherload to grab out the word and get it spelled
close enough? Or are you sitting there thinking the
dick could be a great-grandfather already, didn't he
live through Crimea at least twice? I promise you,
addressing you in my guise as an irridentist in good
standing, I couldn't get to first base without taking
what looks untaken left and right.

As in what d'you got?

I work that out right?

Or whaddaya?

Not to fail to notice who's already typing columnar-
style.

For to effect the gobble effect, ja?

Gobbling up the other guy's paper – crowding the
other guy out.

Watch this.

You watching?

Egress's.

Paper of *Egress*.

Do I care?

It's what them tories get when they have had the
cheek to have situated themselves in the motherland
and given the rebs to know you produce for them a
piece by the fifteenth of August or you (me, Gordo!)
can go fly a kite.

You understand what I'm saying to you?

Because I am saying to you I ever so bargingly asked and was answered by way of harsh reply: 'Make sure we have it in hand for diagetic consultation by the cut-off date or go wait in line like everybody else!'

Excuse me.

WAIT, you say?

For *Egress* 3, you say?

Twiddle my arthritic thumbs whilst the world of worldwide literation passes me by?

Hey.

So did I or didn't I already sequester for myself a second page yet?

Yeah, yeah – *Egress* – sure, sure.

How many pages?

How much paper?

Eat it, polity! – what you're seeing is freedom's dandy doodling here.

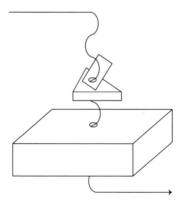

WAYNE HOGAN

I DON'T GET IT

All right, pipe down, calm down, settle down, quit it with all the rustleage of paper, here cometh a little something for your head-piece, it being no little something (not your head-piece, mind you, nobody's belittling your head-piece, your head-piece is probably pretty okay for the time being) for you to make room for up inside of it up there up on top of the mental pedestal where you already better got Gorey and Baxter and Steed life-wise displayed. That's it. Enough said. A word to the wise is maybe still sufficient.

LOVE AND KISSES, GORDO

THE FIRST PRESBYTERIAN.

Wayne Hogan

AN IDLE HOUR IN FINLAND.

A SMALL HITCH
IN THE GROWTH OF THE MATERIAL WORLD.

Wayne Hogan

THE FINE ART OF SHIPBUILDING.

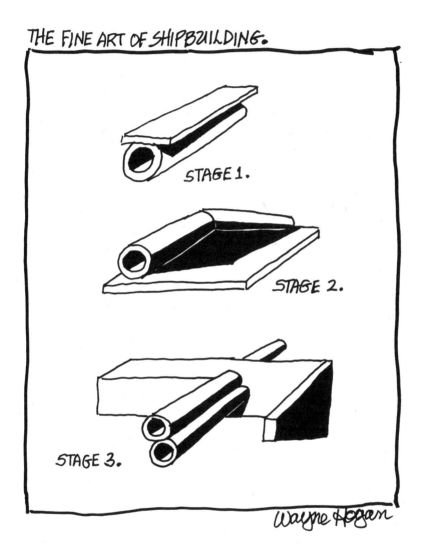

STAGE 1.

STAGE 2.

STAGE 3.

Wayne Hogan

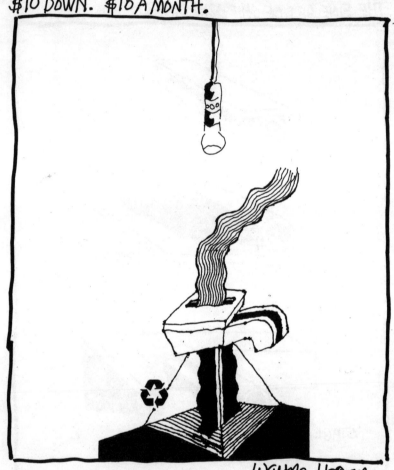

FRANCE BEFORE NAPOLEON.

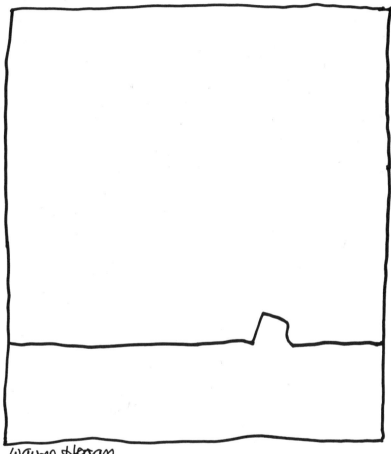

Wayne Hegan

DON'T TRY THIS AT HOME.

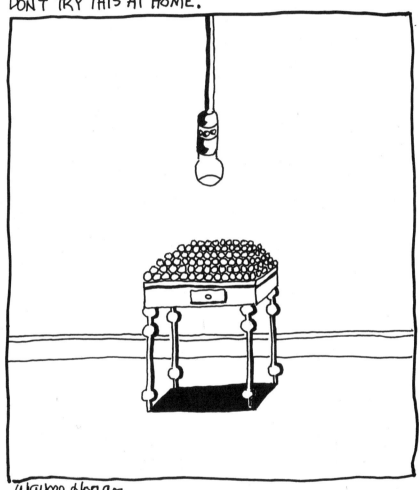

Wayne Hogan

FIRST EVER GRAPHIC POEM.

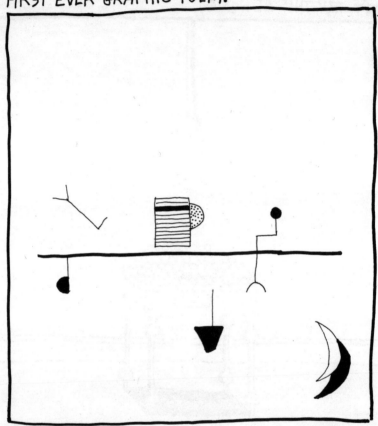

Wayne Hogan

FINALLY—SOMETHING THAT MEANS SOMETHING!

Wayne Hogan

NOT EVEN SOCIOLOGY CAN EXPLAIN THIS.

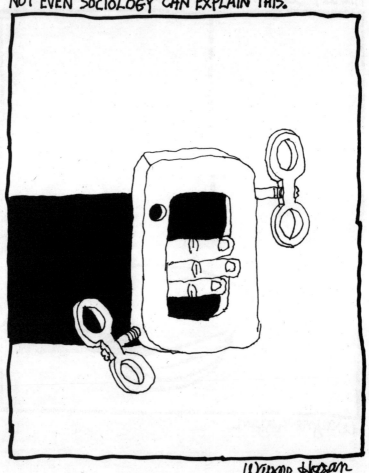

Wayne Hogan

THE SHAPE OF THINGS TO COME.

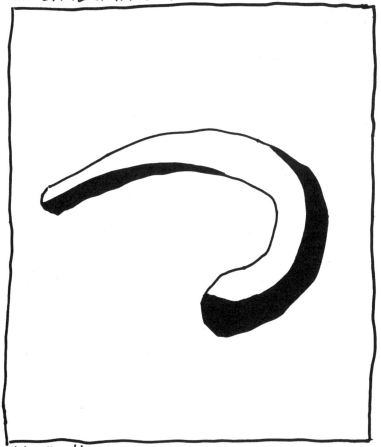

Wayne Hogan

THIS IS KIND OF OBVIOUS.

Wayne Hogan

PHILOSOPHY MADE SIMPLE.

Wayne Hogan

LOGICAL EXTENSION OF KANTIAN AESTHETICS.

Wayne Hogan

THE GO-TO STEPS TO EQUILATERAL SURCEASE.

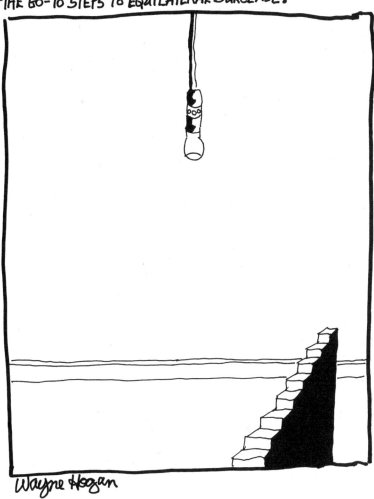

Wayne Hogan

POST-HUMAN.

Wayne Hogan

Lily Hackett

Two Fictions

ICEBOX

Fish egg, suspect, big as a hen's is. Mag sicked savoury cream in the basement of the restaurant. Flabby blinis. 'A vagrant talked up this joint to me,' said Bad. 'My guts belong to you,' she said. A puck of minced chicken in dill sauce – you know the rest. Petit vodkas scented with gingerbread and melon. She was sick again in the street. 'Eighty for you to throw it all up,' he said. In Kazakhstan he'd rode bikes through the night. 'All your stories start with you cutting an onion,' he said. Mag was embarrassed. 'I'm trying to make you cry,' she said.

'I'd like to visit the Bastille tomorrow,' she said.

'It's not there.'

'I know.'

'Even if it was,' he said, 'what we thought were its cruellest oubliettes were just the rooms they kept the ice cool in. Most prisoners kept suites.'

'Sade!' she said.

Man the man Bad had a temper. On the last of the long weekend he half-handed her in anger, and then it was leave or wait and see if he would ever hit for real. She went to Aunt Maw to work it out. During that time Mag couldn't do emulsions; made a nemesis of hollandaise, cocked up vinaigrette. 'You must be on your period,' said Aunt Maw, fey, brim with cottage knowledge. Mag wished Bad was her baby son, so none could say she loved him too much. During that fantasy she boiled apples to mash and was extra careful with the salt. Whenever she could be bothered to brown the beef, she did it for him. She was never full, felt full of gusts like a drum. Ate swelling things like couscous and white rice, hoped it would grow in her. Then ate anything really and most. Aunt Maw sent her into the park to eat clover. 'Is it a remedy?' said Mag. 'It's economy,' said Aunt Maw. 'I can't afford you'.

'You can't just be concerned with your own pain,' said Bad through the wires. 'I miss you very much.' There were many sad things in the park that day and Mag only one of them. Six girls walked with their arms linked, and one girl in the same uniform was limping to keep up. A man tore cinema reviews from a free magazine. After that it was all sad, even the pretty nannies on the benches. On her knees for the clover eating, Mag's eyes welled, made errors. Like how she thought a man had tissue stuck to his shoe, but it was his white dog walking to heel, rind of melon appeared as roadkill, and a baby was thrown into the lido but was just a sack of plastics. There was a man who wore an orange jumper. She could tell he was mad by his circular walk. 'Hello,' she said. 'What is in your life? And do you have any restaurant recommendations?' He showed green teeth, beautiful, like a cool tiled room.

'Madwoman,' he said.

'Bampot,' she said.

'Window-licker'.

'Icebox!'

Was she tiled like that inside? She ran tests to check. She ate ice cubes and they all came out water. Relief. She could keep Bad harmless there. All she had of him she put into the oubliette. Ate a white slice of mattress. Ate the holiday money. Pumped his chamomile soap onto her tongue. She didn't eat the photos, but took photos of the photos and so removed the soul of them. She ate ash out of the rucksack. 'Some women eat dirt when they're pregnant,' said Aunt Maw. 'I'm not,' said Mag, 'remember the gribiche I split.' When she was full, it was sweet to be full, and she went out into the road with her mouth open so a little light could touch him. The madman was laid curled in the centre of the road, eating an icy lolly. There was a crowd. He was refusing his removal. Because his mouth was side-on to the lolly, there were blue juices down his neck. 'I saw this man in Beirut. He told me where to go for best venison,' said Bad from the oubliette. Mag belched the sentence: a dish never eaten, suddenly remembered.

That's how it was at first: everyone birthdayish and furtive, smirking. The snow had keened people to each other, everyone chapped, sluttish to the touch.

'There's blood on your philtrum,' said Doll to the girl.

'My what?' said the girl, dabbling at her plate.

'Your cleft,' said Doll, thumbing her own.

The girl pushed her tongue up to it, left it wet. 'Not mine,' she said and turned away, pleased, curving into her phone to tell whoever it was that she had worn their blood to work. This was new, a snow-thing, girls staggering in on Fridays with hymns in their eyes, to sit sorely on inflatable rubber rings. The magazines told of a woman who:

> found my lover's nails intolerably long and often he would scratch me something silly. Today he came home with cold red hands and said to me put them into the heat of your sucking mouth and warm me. I did, taking each finger in turn, and when I reached the tip, I took the nail in my mouth and bit it clean away! Spat it out like pith.

And a man who:

> pushed my whole wee self, Rock Hard, into a drift!

Big men then began pressing themselves tenderly into banks of snow, in teams of three or four, to see who could stay hardest for longest. Some even came, or pretended to, and caught it on video. She sent one to him, said, 'you would never manage this.' He had told her before that he liked how she was warm, and would hold his hand against her in the minutes after, even though she complained that it rattled her. He replied, after a time, 'I could do that actually,' and she wondered why she was always putting her life in his mouth.

Even if the letters were lies, the tube trains too were rotten with longing. The magazines even had a name for it. But it didn't need a name, this process of going cold and colder at the end of a light, wide Wednesday. The bars were full of office boys and girls ordering Picpoul and salad Nicoise, the girls bluing and beautiful in cheap smocks. And if someone brushed someone else's breast or back on their long stretch for the ice, the whole young group felt it as if a clean penny had been dropped into their cotton thongs. Doll went after work, ordered lettuce and coleslaw, waited until her fingers went numb, and then tried to text him.

He had told her he wanted to see 'her London' but there was no point in going to galleries with him. The art had been stranged by the weather, gone dumb and muttony. In every gallery, even the small ones, there were pictures of buses in the snow, phone booths in the snow, grainy photos of gardens in the snow, snowmen with wilting noses. Every new sculpture was an ice sculpture, every show showcased swans holding lovehearts, swans kissing other swans, lit from below and within with pink bulbs. She decided instead she would show him all the hot brass guns and ambulance blankets, touch his cock through the cloth of his jeans in every room of the museum.

On the seventh Thursday since the snow, Doll was eating carrot cake with tahini frosting. He texted her, said, 'I want to see your Kent too.'

The girl had cut a long neat slit into her arm and was using a pen to poke open where it was scabbing over. 'I'm washing it in the river tonight,' said the girl. 'She's got one too, matching. We are doing it together. It's like when you drink vodka from the freezer, only better. Last time she stopped breathing altogether.'

'There's snow on the roads, though,' Doll texted back. At half-past she went into the bathroom, took off her bra , felt the sit of her breasts under her viscose top. She walked home, holding her body alongside the chafe, chasing the same white pain the girl was chasing, red poppies blooming into the fabric. But in her room, when she unstuck the top from the red crusts where her chest had bled, the hurt was small and already purpling, growing richer by the minute as it reached room-temperature. She was too fleshy to play this game, too fat and lovely, made to be wreathed in leaf and chiffon. It was enormous outside, enormously yellow and near.

'This cold will raw you,' she texted him, 'leave you trembling like an egg.'

'I'll text you,' he texted back. She wanted to explain about the planes, wanted to make him afraid.

They slid across the width of the runway, and the best slides made the news. She liked watching the people pour out of the doors, swaying in line, happy to be alive, grateful to the pilots, and no, there was no snow in Seville yet, nor in Orly. She let the small fantasy of his plane-death play out in her mind, allowing for the thick split of the engines, the long puppet of his recovered body. The deep grief, the platters of sashimi in the funeral's buttery.

The thaw came in the morning, all at once, washed and glossy. Nothing on the news except foreign horrors. A ripe, fresh city pushed up like a mushroom, with the clean earth smell of a mushroom, sporing buses and houses and boys in suits, walking upright for the first time in months. Doll's building was full, and the bodies there were washed like the pavement, with wet hair and the smell of coconut conditioner. Everyone was packety, new, creased with newness. The kitchen had been cleaned overnight and small, threatening notices had appeared. Now the girl's wound was stitched and blooming. It didn't look neat now but mushroomed too, bigger, dark, luscious with bruise-blood.

'She tried to kill me,' said the girl.

'Excuse me?' said Doll.

'Last night, by the river. We were on the kerb of it, where it's a whole beach of plastic, and when I went to dip the slit, she pushed me, dumped the weight of me in it.'

'How did it feel?'

'Cold, really cold. Now it's warmer we're thinking of not touching each other, at least not until summer. When she saw I was alive she put me in tinfoil and we planned it out. We'll go to the gym and watch each other in the weight-room, push further into deeper dips than ever, and after, in bed, like I said, not touch each other, ever, until summer.'

'Do you fear her?'

'Very much!' the girl grinned, and her teeth were chipped where cold had chattered them.

At the end of the day the room was still full, full at six, and at half six still full. The emails at seven were getting desperate, and the sign-offs were shy. Doll walked home in darkness, nothing left to reflect the halogen glare. The shops were full of families and she wondered where they had been, what they had been eating these last white weeks. The magazines were all talking, naming it again. That would be summer, then, a soaked city, all lying sweating in bed, hard and mad. She saw the girl's lover in every article, muscles thick and still, frozen with a hand half-raised to rape or murder.

When he came, she would hurry to touch him. It would all be touch and she would birth in him a love for her like a lamb, a blooded, stumbling love. Ringed in with high pylons, he would never go beyond the green of her bed, no art, just touch, tap-water and a pack of dry crackers. Later, in the summer, she would bring his love to slaughter, eat it like a runt's mother, and in this she would go further than any other cut-hungry Londoner. Watching his flight on the on-line tracker, she spread boy's blue hair gel through her hair. She dressed in an imitation flight suit, stiff with zippers, pockets all over, each less than a finger deep. Laced up stiff boots too, buffed them with cloth and breath. She waited for morning, the thaw now final and flawless. The tubes were full and the papers print-ed cardio tips and apologies for the smut of the letters.

The tunnels pressed her deeper and under, under the water of the spilling river. Under the silent heights, the city sweating out its fever, pouring its love and com-ings into the gutters. Under the sky, the new blue sky, fuel blue, dense with jets and failing jet engines, stut-tering over London. Under hostesses in berets saying brace, brace. Under him again, under the safety of his chosen plane, which cannot land because of the crash, and is circling, circling, again and again. Him a fixed point in the distance; her coming fast, rushing up to meet him.

Michael Cuglietta

In the Middle of the Ocean

I figured as long as she was talking, she wasn't drowning.

I went to the mini bar and fixed myself a drink. It was before sunrise.

When I returned to the bathroom, she was quiet.

I put my drink down and searched for something I could use to break in. The fire axe in the hallway.

In the closet, I found a wire coat hanger. I straightened out the tip and stuck it in the hole in the doorknob.

She was asleep. The water was pouring over the side of the tub, collecting on the tile floor. I turned off the water and unplugged the drain.

I lifted her from under her arms. She felt like ice. As I was trying to wrap a towel around her, she woke up.

'Get your hands off me.' She ran out of the bathroom.

'Slow down. You'll slip and break your neck.'

'Stop telling me what to do.' She was by the mini bar, trying to unscrew a bottle of Heineken, naked with soapsuds dripping everywhere.

'That's a pry off,' I told her.

She found the bottle opener and took it out to the balcony. I waited a couple of minutes and, when I was sure she wasn't coming back, went out after her.

She was reclined on the lounge chair, her beer propped up next to her. Her eyes were closed. When I got close, I saw her lips were blue. 'You have to come inside.' I leaned in and touched her shoulder. She came to life.

She waved her bottle at me, spraying beer in my face. When all the beer was gone, she threw the bottle. I ducked just in time. It shattered against the wall behind me.

She walked through the broken glass and into the cabin, slamming the sliding door shut. She tried to lock me out but she was too drunk. She went to the mini-bar, got another beer and settled on the couch.

I leaned over the railing and looked down at the water.

I went back inside. She was snoring. I slid the bottle out of her hand. Then took the comforter off the bed and laid it on top of her. I went into the shower. The hot water felt good running down my shoulders and back. When I was done, I put on a pair of shorts and a white t-shirt and set out for the dining hall.

There was a father and son in the cabin next to ours. When I walked past, the son appeared in the doorway.

'Here he is, dad.' He wore only a pair of swim trunks. He was tall and thin. His chest hollow, like a bird.

I put my head down and kept walking.

'We heard you this morning,' he called after me as I was getting in the elevator. 'Does it make you feel like a big man, beating up on a woman?'

There was a woman in the elevator with me. She grabbed her daughter and held her close. I kept my eyes on the floor.

I stopped on deck to have a cigarette. Then went to the breakfast buffet. I filled my plate with eggs, bacon, hash browns and pancakes. A waitress came around with a pot of coffee. I drank three cups and left the food untouched.

There were a couple of security guards eating at the table next to me. As I walked out, I gave them a nod.

On a cruise, there's no judge or jury, just a holding tank in the bowels of the ship.

After a couple more cigarettes on deck, I walked to the back of the boat and watched the crew guide us into port.

When I booked the cruise, I signed up for the snorkeling excursion in Mexico. The brochure had a picture of a young couple floating in the middle of the ocean. The woman wore a tiny blue bikini that showed off her ass. A man swam behind her, a big smile on his face.

Cathy Sweeney

The Birthday Present

For his fifty-seventh birthday I bought my husband a sex doll. It cost a lot of money, but I'd been saving for years. I work part-time in a school for adolescents with special needs and that's where I first encountered sex dolls when one was bought for a teenage boy with *Klüver-Bucy Syndrome*. The medication to reduce the boy's sex drive made him sick and so the psychiatrist prescribed a sex doll. It made me think of my husband who also has a strong sex drive.

I am a practical woman – I wear my hair short and don't bother with make-up – and so I told my husband about his present weeks before his birthday. Sex dolls are in huge demand and you need to place your order at least a month prior to delivery. According to the website, summertime is almost as busy as Christmas, and my husband's birthday was in July. The manufacturing company are based in San Diego, but they have a European outlet. Also, it is not just a case of clicking a mouse and ordering one. Sex dolls are made to specification, no two are exactly alike, and there are lots of choices to make before an order can be processed – nipple preference, labia style, hair colour, chest measurement, ethnicity, and so on. More choices than when we installed our new kitchen. My husband was never a decisive man, so in the end, with him slouched beside me on the couch, I scrolled through images from the website on my laptop and coaxed the choices out of him. Some surprised me – a smaller sized breast with a darker nipple – and some didn't – Caucasian, blonde, blue eyes.

We had a good marriage but over the years I had grown to dislike sex with my husband. It was not his desire that I objected to. I could understand that. The girls in the school where I work are put on the pill as soon as they turn fourteen. What I objected to was my husband turning me into an object to suit his own needs. In those last years I became an expert at separating mind from body while my husband panted above me – thinking about what bulbs to plant in the garden, or a programme I had seen on TV, or how to cook the leftover lamb in the fridge.

The doll arrived as ordered on my husband's birthday. I had given him a gardening book over breakfast but told him that his real present would be waiting for him when he got home that evening. I took time off work to take the delivery. It was particularly warm while I sat in the living room watching the road, and I was irritated by the buzzing of flies. It was a relief when a plain white van pulled up outside the house. The box was so large that the delivery man had to wheel it up the driveway. He had a look on his face which said I know exactly what this is, but he made no comment and I signed the electronic pad and that was that. The amount of packaging was criminal. I filled two bags for recycling.

The doll was dressed in a see-through nightdress with matching panties, white over-the-knee socks and a pair of black patent high heeled shoes. I carried her upstairs to the guest bedroom, which was no mean feat as she weighed about seven stone. In my hands her silicone skin felt spongy. Her eyes opened and closed like a toy and she smelled faintly of plastic. I bumped her head off the door jamb but there was no response. I had installed the app on my husband's phone, but she hadn't been activated yet. The technology was amazing. The current generation of sex dolls can talk, simulate sex noises and responses, and even swivel their hips and bottom. They can't walk or make facial expressions yet, but it is only a matter of time.

In the previous weeks I had decorated the guest bedroom. Originally, it had been my son's room, but he'd moved to Toronto to set up a company marketing smart technology in the work place. It was doing well, and Tom worked round the clock. My daughter's room was further down the landing. Stephanie was the creative one in the family and was in London designing stage sets for a small theatre company. Her room was exactly as she had left it the last time she moved out, although I had cleaned it.

I painted the walls of the guest bedroom a warm reddish colour and bought a thick pile rug for the floor and a new cream-coloured blind for the window. I also bought an expensive scented candle and a new mattress for the bed, an orthopaedic one, as my husband suffered from lumbago, especially in winter. I lay the doll on the bed, fixed her hair and clothing, pulled down the blind, lit the candle and waited for my husband to come home from work. When he saw Tina – that was the name we had chosen for the doll – the skin on his neck reddened and his eyes flushed with excitement.

Most evenings, and sometimes on weekend mornings, my husband would visit Tina. He always sought me out afterwards, cuddling me a little if I was watching TV, or popping his head around the door if I was in the kitchen or watering plants on the patio, just letting me know, I suppose, that the visit was over, and waiting for me to say something. Was that nice, love? Good. Would like some coffee? My husband became more attentive to me, buying me flowers and fetching errands without being asked. He even lost a little weight and wheezed less in his sleep

I worked in the school for adolescents with special needs on Tuesdays, Wednesdays and Thursdays. Monday was my day for cleaning the house and on Fridays I went shopping. Weekends my husband and I spent together. My Monday routine changed after Tina arrived, but I didn't mind. I left cleaning her room until last, when there was nothing else to do, so that I could take my time. I'd put Tina sitting in the chair while I stripped the bed and dusted and vacuumed. Then I would place a rubber backed towel – I took one from work – on the mattress, and lie Tina on it, and undress her and sponge her down from top to toe with a warm soapy cloth, first her back and then her front, making sure I gently wiped everywhere, before inserting a small irrigator into her vagina, anus and mouth, and drying her with a facecloth. Then I would take a freshly laundered outfit from the wardrobe, maybe the red lace set with suspender belt or the black corset with crotch-less panties. My husband and I ordered something new online every month or so. Lastly, I'd dress her, brush her hair, put fresh linen on the bed and arrange her on it

As autumn closed in and the streetlights began to come on earlier and earlier, I developed a habit of lighting the candle and slipping off my shoes and lying on the bed beside Tina, not doing anything, just thinking. Sometimes I thought about all the rooms people had in their houses – kitchens and sitting rooms and bedrooms – and how in each room you're expected to do something – eat or relax or sleep – but in this room there was nothing to do, and how nice that was, especially with the feeling of not being completely on your own, of being with someone who was not going to ask you to do anything, just let you lie there, watching the shadows of the leaves of the tree outside the window flicker back and forth on the window blind.

I was in the supermarket when I got the phone call. It must have been a Friday. I remember that the shelves were full of Christmas decorations and *You'd better watch out, you'd better not cry* was playing on the Tannoy system. I was just about to take a packet of salmon darnes from the fridge when my phone rang. I thought salmon would make a nice change from pork chops and I was thinking of serving them on a bed of creamed potatoes with maybe asparagus or tender stemmed broccoli, whatever was freshest. The phone call was from the Garda station. They wanted to know if I was Mrs Susan Nugent, if I was the wife of Robert Nugent, if I lived at Cherryfield Drive, The Glen, Dublin 4, if my husband drove a silver Toyota Mondeo 161 D 1672. I was beginning to lose patience when the voice on the other end told me there'd been an accident involving my husband and I needed to go to St. Vincent's Hospital straightaway. She said a Garda unit had called to the house, but no one had been there. I thanked the voice and hung up. I thought I'd better not buy the salmon darnes after all since I wouldn't eat both, and salmon makes a terrible smell in the fridge. Then I wondered what I do with the rest of the shopping in my trolley. A boy with bad acne was packing shelves at the far end of the aisle and I tried explaining to him what had happened, but his English was poor, and he couldn't understand, so in the end I just abandoned the trolley and walked out of the supermarket and drove to the hospital.

An Indian doctor told me my husband was dead. He spoke very softly. My husband had suffered a cardiac arrest while driving to work. He had been pronounced dead at 7.23 am. There were no other vehicles involved. No one else was hurt. He had collapsed at the wheel while parked at a traffic light in Donnybrook. An ambulance had brought him to the hospital but there was nothing they could do. His car had been temporarily impounded. A nurse took my down a corridor and into a small room where my husband was laid out on a metal trolley with a sheet over him, just like on TV. The nurse was very kind and kept asking if I'd prefer to wait until a family member or a friend was with me, but I said no, I'd prefer to identify my husband on my own. She pulled the sheet down. Although his jaw was slack and the colour had gone from his skin, he looked as if he was sleeping. I smiled at the nurse Yes, that's him, that's my husband. Yes, Robert Nugent. Then we left him there, lying in the white room, sleeping peacefully.

The funeral is a blur. I know everyone says that, but they probably say it because it is true. It's like being in a play. You have lines to say. So sad. Thank you. He was too young. Enjoying life. Thank you. And you have cues for entering and exiting churches, funeral parlours, graveyards, hotels. And then suddenly it is over and you are back in your own bed in your own house, except that now you are alone. In the coffin my husband looked like the corpse of a middle-aged man. Grey and stiff. He was no longer sleeping. He was dead.

Tom and Stephanie took the first available flights home for the funeral. Stephanie wore jeans, saying she hadn't anything else with her, while Tom, who had brought only a sports bag, wore a suit and dark tie. Stephanie slept in her own room, but I made up a bed for Tom in the study. I explained that some of dad's things were being stored in his old room. I had locked the door of the guest bedroom and put the key in a secret compartment of my jewellery box. Two days after the funeral Tom returned to Toronto. His flight was at some unearthly hour, so he ordered a taxi to take him to the airport. Stephanie said she would stay a bit longer and quickly settled into her old habits of sleeping late in the mornings and sloping around the house in pyjamas bottoms and sweatshirts.

On Christmas day we ate dinner on our laps while watching TV. I did all the cooking. After a few glasses of wine, Stephanie got teary, saying how much she missed daddy, and fell asleep on the couch. I did the cleaning up as quietly as I could so as not to wake her. I put the radio on in the kitchen. I am not a religious person but I like listening to choirs singing from churches. When Ave Maria came on I sat at on a stool at the marble counter listening to the music echoing around the kitchen, tears thickening my eyes even though I didn't feel sad.

In the new year I returned to work. When I'd come home, there'd be bits of Stephanie in every room: a hoodie in the kitchen, her handbag in the hall, her phone charging on the mantlepiece, a cold cup of coffee on the worktop, a magazine left open on the couch. Sometimes, at night, watching TV or lying in bed with the electric blanket on, I'd think of Tina in the guest bedroom. I hadn't unlocked the door since the day I'd come home from the hospital. I didn't want to go in there until I had the house to myself again.

One day in mid-January Stephanie phoned me while I was at work to say she had made dinner. She said it would be nice for me to put my feet up and that there was something she wanted to talk to me about. Dinner was spaghetti bolognaise. I tried not to eat too much as garlic always repeats on me. Stephanie said that she was thinking about changing career, becoming a dressmaker. She said it made sense to stay in Dublin and work from home. And that was what she wanted to talk to me about. Tom's old room. Since it wasn't being used –

'No,' I said.

'No?' Her voice was thin and high. 'Is that it? Just no?'

'No.'

My own voice, I noticed, was surprisingly steady, and I kept my hands folded on my lap just in case they started shaking.

'Unbelievable.' Stephanie got up from the table. 'Un-fucking-believable.'

'Don't –

'I get it. I'll be out of here as soon as I can.'

Two months later Stephanie was still there.

I went to see a solicitor to arrange a small inheritance from my husband's savings to be released to both Tom and Stephanie. I gave each of them the same amount. I received an email from Tom the next day saying thank you. He added that he was planning to marry his girlfriend in Bali. I wasn't sure which girlfriend he was referring to, but I emailed back congratulations.

On the morning that Stephanie left to return to her job in London, I dropped her to the airport. In the departure lounge we hugged and she promised to Skype me once a week. I could smell her freshly shampooed hair and feel the outline of her shoulder blades, and for a moment I almost asked her to stay. Then she released herself from me, gave one big wave, and was gone.

On the way back from the airport the sky was deep blue like it was full of something. The roads glinted in the early morning light and the first signs of spring were visible along the edges of the motorway. It struck me that people can stay the same for a very long time and then they can change very quickly. It seemed like a very long time ago that I had bought my husband a birthday present.

When I got home I went straight upstairs and un-locked the door of the guest bedroom. The room was freezing, so I left my coat on. Tina was cold. Her skin felt like chilled jelly. A fly was rattling around inside the lampshade on the bedside locker. I unplugged the lamp and opened the window and shook the lamp so hard that the fly flew out and disappeared into the air. I closed the window and set the lamp up again and put the heating on. Then I went into Stephanie's room and took and old pair of sweatpants and a hoodie and a pair of knickers from her chest of drawers. I took a pair of woollen socks from the hot press. I filled a ba-sin of warm soapy water and put the rubber sheet on the bed and lay Tina on it and washed her from top to toe as carefully and thoroughly as I could. There was a stale milky odour from her vagina. When I was done

I patted her dry and dressed her in the clothes. Then I changed the sheets on the bed and hoovered and dusted and replaced the candle with one that a neighbour had given me for Christmas and lit it. I found my husband's phone and activated the app for Tina and put in on the *Innocent* setting.

'How are you today?' I asked her.

'I am very well,' she answered.

'You look nice.'

'Thank you. So you do.'

'That's a nice thing to say,' I said. 'Would you like to take a nap?'

'If you like.' She closed her eyes. 'If you like.'

I turned off the app and put the phone on the bedside locker. Then I covered Tina's legs with a fleece blanket and slipped off my shoes and lay on the bed beside her, still with my coat on. The room was warm and smelled of cinnamon. Later – since it was Friday – I'd go shopping, but just for a while I'd relax and let the weight of my body sink into the bed while the shadows of the leaves on the tree outside rippled back and forth on the window blind in a million shades of grey, as though they were real leaves, and not just the shadows of them.

Brad Phillips

The Barista, the Rooster & Me

A woman hasn't seen her son for six years after kicking him out of the house for stealing money for drugs. To deal with the loss of her son, the mother ends up finding comfort in those same drugs. One day, needing to get high, she walks to the spot where she always buys dope. Instead of her usual dealer beckoning her into the doorway of the bar, she realizes that the man taking her money is her son.

A man is in Houston on business. He hasn't had sex with his wife in over two years. He isn't the type of man to pay for sex when he travels. This time, frustration with his marriage combined with his neglected sex drive overpower his sense of morality. Flipping through the back of a free local newspaper he finds the escort ads. Hot college girls who will do anything. Fresh-faced. Will wear school uniform if requested. So naive as to think the body in the photo is the body of the girl who will arrive at his door, he nervously places the call, empties half the mini-bar and waits. After an hour there's a knock at the door. He doesn't want to answer it. He's changed his mind. But that's not an option. He opens the door. It takes him more than a minute – but not her, who's begun crying – to realize the girl standing in his hotel room wearing a cheap orange dress with a neck tattoo is his daughter Alicia, who he hasn't seen since she left home to begin her sophomore year at school.

Worried he'll be late for work and gunning for a promotion, a young father doesn't properly check his rear-view mirror, slowly reversing over his four-year old son, who is *struggling to learn to ride a bike with training wheels.*

Traveling to Jordan to visit a dying aunt, a chemical engineering student finds himself duct-taped to a chair in a room that exists on no maps, only six hours after landing in his homeland for the first time.

A family of four wins one-hundred-eighty million dollars in the lottery.

Taking a long train trip across the country to treat herself and relax, a recently-widowed woman is unable to sleep in her private car. She is traveling through nothing but flat, endlessly replicating prairie. She cups her hands to the window and presses her nose to the glass, attempting to get a look at what's speeding by her. After a minute, passing before her so quickly she'll spend the rest of her life questioning whether or not it truly happened, she sees a bald man in a white jumpsuit standing only a few feet from the tracks, staring into the windows. In that nanosecond, they make eye contact.

$\bullet\ \bullet\ \bullet$

The night before I got shipped off to live with strange men for a year, Paul, one of my roommates, found me at the bottom of the stairs when he came home from the casino. I was a six foot tall confusion of limbs and paper white skin lying crumpled at the bottom of a staircase. My memory is fuzzy, but I remember Paul kicked me in the stomach and waited until my eyes found his. He asked if I could spare a cigarette then laughed obnoxiously and walked into the kitchen.

He laughed because I was naked and obviously didn't have any cigarettes.

I felt my face and I knew something was wrong. I recalled my friend Jeremy peeling me off Hastings Street, insisting that I stop what I was doing.

'Just stay down. Stay down or come with me. Don't go back for more.'

I remember going back for more.

I remember the sound it made inside my head when the bouncer cracked my face on the wall, breaking my orbital bone. I remember understanding that this was why my face felt wrong. I remember being scared to look in the mirror. I don't remember how I got home, but I did.

I'd packed my bags early that morning, knowing that I only had one day left to get fucked up; one day left before I got shipped off to live with the strange men for a year. I'd had one day left and I wanted to use it. Based on my broken face, I guessed I did.

The van that came to get me had three guys in it, all of them tough-looking dummies. I remember thinking, 'These guys are dummies.' I remember the driver saying 'Oh fuck' when he saw me. I think they carried me down the front stairs of the house and helped me into the van. One of them must have taken my bag. I remember my roommate Paul when I looked back. He gave me the finger and smiled.

The strange men were taking me to what people call rehab. Rehab is not what people in rehab call rehab.

We call it treatment. Being in treatment was the first time I ever saw the good in men. It was a unifying environment; not only because we were all addicts, or addicts trying to get well, but because each one of us, no matter what our story, found ourselves together because of things that had happened in our lives – those things from which we could not return.

The stories I have of that year are innumerable.

The following few help me explain why today I find myself struggling so hard to deal with a problem I've been having – a problem I've been having with the sensitive barista who lives beneath my wife, Cristine, and I in a way where nobody ends up hurt, or in jail.

One story I have is about Mike. Mike was a sweetheart First Nations man who moved with me from the hospital to the halfway house where I lived for nine months. On weekends we were allowed to go to the community centre, where we'd all swim. It was the only time that nobody was breathing down our necks. Mike had gotten his stomach stapled years before, and it always broke my heart to see him in the pool in a loose black t-shirt. There was a sweet fat kid who would come with us who also wore a t-shirt in the pool, but with Mike I knew it was because he was ashamed of whatever his skin looked like underneath, which for some reason felt more sad to me.

Mike was always quiet. Like a lot of people I came to know that year, he would always make sure that wherever he was in a room, nobody could get behind him. It was almost funny in group therapy the way there'd be so much empty space, every single guy sitting in a chair pressed up against the wall. Prison habits are hard to break I guess.

Mike came to treatment three years after getting out of the penitentiary, where he'd spent twelve years for second-degree murder. He'd been with his two young daughters one weekend near Christmas. He took them shopping and when they exited the mall, Mike put a fresh hundred-dollar bill in a Salvation Army kettle. As he walked away, he looked back and saw the guy with the kettle carefully extract the hundred and slip it into his pocket. Mike told his daughters to wait in the car, then he took a crowbar from the floor of his back seat and slowly walked back towards the mall.

Mike said he remembered nothing, but later discovered he'd killed the guy by hitting him in the head and face with the crowbar over twenty times.

He would cry in group therapy when he told us how his daughters screamed when he came back to them covered in blood. He didn't know he was covered in blood, because he was blackout drunk. The police picked him up before he left the parking lot.

Another story I have is about Danny. Danny moved into our halfway house after I'd been there a while. Of everyone I met there, he was the one I felt most drawn to. Danny was a bald, fifty-year old longshoreman who'd never been clean for more than a few months since the age of nine. He laughed like a cartoon villain at inappropriate moments. He was illiterate. Outside of cleaning and going to 12 step meetings, Danny and I spent a lot of empty time in the house together, so I used some of mine to help him learn to read. Danny was sort of like a child. An insane child, but nonetheless a child.

Danny had never owned a computer before, and the house PC had blocks on it that restricted our access to porn and gambling websites.

Enter Dave, the last house manager we had. Dave, who would sometimes bring his one-legged meth-head girlfriend over on weekends to fuck in his bedroom with the door open, was far more relaxed about rules than the previous managers. Marcello, another guy in the house, had a friend who sold used laptops and Dave didn't care if we all had one.

Danny wanted one. I thought I could use it to help him learn to read. Danny called computers 'the porn machines', and at first I thought he was kidding. I soon learned that he truly didn't know they served any other function outside of putting pornography in front of your face.

So Marcello got him a laptop and Danny opened it one night while the rest of were about to drive to an NA meeting. He looked at it and held it like a monkey might hold an hourglass. He claimed total confusion as to how it worked. Someone said, 'You'll figure it out Dan.' And when we got back from the meeting two hours later, there he was in the living room, placidly watching something I'd never seen before: Russian anorexic porn. I glimpsed the cock of a young comrade visibly poking up through the atrophied pelvic muscles of a far too thin girl. Someone asked Danny, 'What the fuck how did you find this?' and he just shrugged. Danny had found a very dark hole online within two hours of finding the power button on the porn machine.

A week before I left, Danny got kicked out. Not for relapsing but for reorganizing Marcello's face using the heavy leg of an oak coffee table he broke off during a fight over control of the television remote.

Through research I've learned that crack addicts enjoy shows like Storage Wars and Duck Dynasty and are inveterate channel flippers, while junkies just want to watch dolphins on the Discovery Channel nonstop.

I was sitting on the pleather sofa, looking at sexual photos of myself and the girl I was seeing when Danny did it. Blood sprayed my laptop and sweater. Nobody in the house wanted to call the cops since they all had police issues, so I called, because it's a drag to watch someone die, and I've miraculously never had trouble with the law. Danny was arrested. I didn't mean for that to happen. It was the last time I saw him.

But there's another story I want to tell about Danny.

Like most longshoremen, Danny made a lot of money and was a crack and heroin addict.

Longshoremen work on call, are unionized and often corrupt, and smoke crack in their trucks collecting double time waiting for something to do. Half the people I met in rehab were either longshoremen or they worked on oil rigs. Too much free time and too much money is bad for the addict brain. Danny used to tell me a lot of stories, and I'd be crying with laughter while he'd ask me what was funny. He thought his life was normal.

A typical day for Danny when he wasn't working was to get four hookers to come to his house and be themselves. He told me the house rules were that as soon as the hookers got there, everyone had to take off their clothes. Then the crack smoking would begin in earnest. He never explained the need for nudity, but it somehow made perfect sense. The hookers were there to fuck, but that was their secondary purpose. Mostly they were there to keep Danny company. He spent more money on crack for them and himself than he did on their hourly rates, and he'd often keep them for the entire weekend. These weren't high end escorts, but he was paying out at least fifty an hour for each girl for 48 hours. Drug math indicates that that's an astonishing amount of rock cocaine.

His life sounded fun. It sounded different than the life of someone married to opiates, which doesn't typically involve hookers. It does often involve getting naked though, but only because you're so fucking sweaty.

Danny had a parrot named Fucker. And besides

dealers and hookers, Danny only had two visitors to his house – his mother and his parole officer. The parrot didn't have many words or sentences to blurt out, because neither did Danny. So his parole officer would drop in, or his mother might bring him a casserole, and Fucker would say one of two things: 'Suck Dan's dick!' and 'Danny wants a hoot! Danny wants a hoot!' The part that cracked me up every time wasn't just what the parrot said, but Danny doing an impersonation of a parrot mimicking his own voice.

Danny would always feel betrayed by Fucker when the PO came, because while he might be able to lie and say he'd been clean, Fucker would let his Parole Officer know that in fact Danny had been asking someone to suck his dick while he was smoking crack. Danny loved Fucker though and even though the bird got his parole revoked and upset his mom, he never spoke ill of it, and kept it until it died.

There is one story that Danny used to tell that has probably taught me the most of all his stories though, and it's epic.

Danny had been working eighty hour weeks for close to six months, and the only time he had to get high and sleep was when he got home at five in the morning. I don't know the bylaws of other cities, but in Vancouver and its environs, you can own chickens and roosters if you use their eggs to feed your family. Two houses down from Danny, a Chinese family owned a particularly robust rooster. Danny would get home, do a small hoot and drink a beer then try to sleep. As he described it, every single morning during those six months, the moment he'd finally settle into sleep, the rooster would start to do its thing. I wish I could type the sound of Danny doing the rooster call. It was convincing and scary. Danny was a short-tempered man to begin with, so add long hours of work and a love affair with crack cocaine, and the rooster soon became Danny's nemesis.

This rooster tested Danny's character. Then one day it pushed him too far. It got inside his head and scratched. He said it took him a lot of crack and prayer to get to the place he needed to get to on that day.

On that fated morning when he got back from work, instead of taking one hoot and trying to sleep, Danny consumed a great deal of crack and rum then took off all his clothes. The nudity is for me both the inscrutable and comic centre of the story. He got his aluminum baseball bat, sat on the edge of his bed, took hit after hit off his pipe, and waited.

Then it came.

When he told the story, at this point Danny would take the rooster sound even further, like something from Revelations. It was Dante's rooster. It was the air siren that signaled the end of the world. Who was brave enough to, instead of cowering in the cellar, leave nude through the sliding glass doors, a bat in one hand, a rum and Coke in the other?

Danny was.

He went outside. He was higher than he'd ever

been. His heart beat, as he said, like 'A Africa drum' in his chest. The sun was barely up. Lights began to come on in the houses around him. Danny, in his horribly pale and pudgy nudity, began to run. Here he would defensively insist that not one drop of his drink spilled. He hopped his fence with bat and drink in hand. He hopped the other. Then there he was, man against bird. Stark naked versus glorious plumage. He sensed the bird knew it was bad. Danny said it took at least twenty minutes of chasing the rooster in circles until the geometry lined up. Then with one swing, propelled by a deep energy going back to his childhood, back to why he smoked crack, in super slow motion the bat came down until it connected with the bird's head, who looked up at him with sad resignation. Danny said the head flew over the fence into the next yard, and while the body twitched, Danny cursed and taunted it. He apparently told the rooster, 'Now you won't fucking coo-coo any fucking coos will you motherfucker.' Then Danny returned to his home the same way he'd came; climbing the fences instead of jumping, enjoying his rum and coke. When he got home though, he walked right through his closed sliding glass doors; then he got into bed bleeding, stuck with shards of glass. Animal control came an hour later, but being a lifelong addict it didn't take long for Danny to charm them into fucking off.

I imagine they were rightfully terrified.

The way Danny tells it you think the story is done there, but it isn't. Danny told us that he had always been a pariah in that neighborhood, and nobody had ever talked to him, but after silencing the beast, he said that every Christmas after that day, when he reached into his mailbox, there would be unsigned hand-delivered letters from people in the neighborhood, thanking him for what he had done.

. . .

Two stories from a year littered with them.

My hope is that they illustrate something. My year in rehab – what I witnessed, what behaviors became familiar to me – returned me to my place of birth forever changed. What transformed inside of me while there constitutes an experience from which I could not return as the Brad Phillips I once was.

People think that getting sober means getting better, becoming a better person.

Sometimes it does, but sometimes it only means getting sober.

My problem five and a half years later, now, is trivial, relative to the constellation of problems I was lost in before, but it's a problem nonetheless.

My problem is with the barista who lives underneath the apartment I share with my wife.

. . .

We moved into our apartment on December 1st. We are quiet people, Cristine and I. While she was in Florida over Christmas, I was watching a movie in bed. Then I heard a knock at my door.

It was eleven at night, and I was watching was *The Verdict* with Paul Newman. If you know this movie you know the only sound is dialogue. When I opened the door a hip twenty-something bro was standing there, his mute girlfriend beside him for support, staring at the ground. He nervously complained about the movie. He said that he had to wake up early for work. Against all instincts surging inside of me, I told him I'd turn the volume down.

He thanked me and left.

A few days later, Cristine was back home and it happened again. This time I stayed in bed – her idea – knowing I would be prone to lose my temper. She spoke to him at the door and returned to me. She told me his name was Jackson. We both laughed.

Jackson styled his hair. Jackson seemed vain. But we loved our new apartment and didn't want to cause any problems, so we began to test out ways to alleviate his distress. We put the speaker on a towel. We put the speaker on a table. Over the following four months, Jackson, who Cristine had by now told to text instead of forcing her out of bed, complained at least ten more times. And each time he would mentioned that he started work early. We were waking him up, Cristine and I, with the speaker turned low and now on our bed, watching the notoriously bass heavy films *Dead*

Ringers and *Barry Lyndon*.

Having only dealt with him that first time, I was developing some serious animosity for Jackson.

Eventually, we found the right volume and he stopped texting us for almost a month. We'd lay in bed, Cristine no longer able to rest her head on my chest as she needed both ears to strain to listen to whatever we were watching with the volume as low as we could manage.

I was not happy with this scenario.

Now my wife is again away. I'm alone, waiting, my mind imagining various scenarios. I want it to happen again.

The previous week I'd gone to the doctor. Cristine, who rarely has time alone in the house, was packing for her trip at two in the afternoon and decided, reasonably to our minds, to listen to Aaliyah with the volume turned up high. Two in the afternoon is a demilitarized zone when it comes to noise. Two in the afternoon is a free for all.

Not for Jackson.

Before the first song was even over, he texted Cristine asking her to please turn the music down. He again mentioned his early rising job, and said that he was trying to get some work done in his apartment. Before, we hadn't known what this taxing job was. Then the information arrived on her phone, strangely to my mind without shame – he told her that he and his partner were *both baristas*. I instantly didn't grasp why he didn't just say they worked at coffee shops. So we'd been, while making art and attempting to write insightful or touching prose and editorial pieces, fucking up the life of a latte artist. No, *two* latte artists. This is why he had to wake up early. To get to the boutique coffee shop. When I got home Cristine was happy and showed me their conversation. We both laughed and said that the work he had to do in his apartment was probably tweaking a vocal track for the demo his band was producing.

She had held her ground though, and told him no. Suck it up, essentially.

She felt better after doing it.

But what Cristine doesn't know is I don't feel better. I feel angry. I feel pissed off that my wife – so quiet, so undemanding – wasn't even given the space to listen to one song while she packed her bag to go on what might be an emotionally difficult trip to see her family.

want Jackson to come back.

I sit here at night, my finger hovering over the volume button on my laptop while I listen to Sonic Youth. Because Jackson is my rooster. A reliably irritating, overly-preened nuisance with no consideration for others. Danny's stories did more than entertain me. They taught me about revenge. They taught about me how to deal with the world extrajudicially.

This is the version of me that has come home. Sober yes, but not improved in all areas. In some ways, worse. I can't encase my anger in an opiate duvet. I can no longer drop it in an endless bottle of Jim Beam. So the only thing saving Jackson today, at 8.27 PM, is that Cristine and I haven't yet found a table we like enough for our apartment. We want something beautiful we'll have for the rest of our lives. That we don't yet have it is the sole reason I'm not turning up the volume tonight, waiting to answer my door, with nothing but a smile and the freshly torn off leg of our new, beautiful Edwardian table.

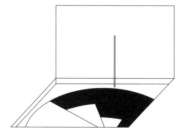

Carrie Cooperider

For Spacious Skies

After I was canned, I couldn't show my face. I didn't know how to act or what to do with myself. And if I thought about it, it had never really been up to me to decide, though, you know? What to do with myself, I mean. I did whatever, because other people were counting on me to do whatever, that's all – did it over and over with pretty much the same result: a regular paycheck, two weeks off a year, and a sad office party whenever the holiday season skulked around. I don't know. Routine, right? But I never liked sleeping in on weekdays, and when I could no longer tell the days apart, I decided to invent an imaginary friend.

I named my friend Mother. She looked like she was about five, maybe a runty six. 'You're a lot younger than I was expecting,' I said. 'Well, I hope you're smarter than you look,' Mother said. She drove some dirt into the living room rug with the toe of her grubby sneaker, pivoting her foot back and forth to grind it in good. She crossed her arms and sighed, looking around but not finding whatever it was. 'You got anything to eat in this dump?' she said. 'I'm starved.'

I made a sandwich on Wonder Bread from mashed canned beans heaped with sugar and a blob of mayo, squished the slices together under my palm, and put it on a paper plate. I was out of napkins. 'Here,' I said, 'bon appetit.' Mother wrinkled her nose so I snatched it back, snipped the crusts off, and butchered it into little triangles. 'Better?' She nodded, tucked in, and I was forced to eavesdrop as she ate. I hate the sounds people make when they mill, moisten, pulp, and gullet their food – me included, though at least I can stop myself mid-chew if it's making me edgy. That stuff should be private. I have a theory about women like me who have to resort to mentally reciting mis-heard song lyrics to drive out the sound of other people eating: we're the ones who never wanted children.

Think about it. The more mouths there are to feed, the more saliva-sloshing (*Oh beautiful for spaceship eyes*), lip-smacking (*for hampered waifs of green*), gastro-gurgling (*for purple-mounted majesties*), tongue-roving (*above the fruitless plain*), throat-burbling (*My Erica! My Erica! Todd gave his grapes to me*), gas-popping (*so crown my cud with motherhood*) soup-slopping (*from sea to Chinese sea*) noise a person has to put up with.

Why would you?

If you're me, you wouldn't – and you didn't.

Mother finished her sandwich and belched. 'What should we play?'

'Play?'

'Got any good toys?'

'I don't have *any* toys.'

'What about in there?' Mother pointed to a door I'd never seen before. It opened to darkness and descending steps. When I flicked the switch on the landing we could see a cement floor and the corner of a table below us. Mother dashed past me toward the mechanical sound that climbed up on the cool air, and I followed her down the stairs.

'Look! It's all set up and moving and everything!' Mother said.

A model train chugged past a graveyard filled with fuzzy humps and hillocks and fake stunted cedars and crazed headstones. 'I'm going to pretend we're on that train,' said Mother, 'going someplace nice for a change. I get dibs on the window seat. We'll play 'I Spy.' Me first. I spy: something white!'

I didn't have anything else to do, so I said: 'Is it the graffiti on the bridge over the tracks with the letters R-I-P?'

'No, it's not flat like that.'

'Is it that plastic bag fluttering from the tree branch?'

'No, it's something the wind can't blow around.'

A pair of stained pastel-pink panties had been pulled over the top of a rounded headstone with the leg holes positioned where ears might have poked out if headstones had ears, in which case the rest of the fabric would have been a blindfold – but the panties were light-colored, not white.

'Is it the top part of the busted streetlight?'

'No, it's not anything above ground.'

'How can you see it, then?' I noticed a group of mourners around an open grave. In it was a tiny white casket. 'Is it a baby-sized coffin?' I asked.

'Yes!' said Mother, laughing and clapping, 'That's it! Your turn!'

Past the cemetery the train glided by a burnt-out

house with its front door agape, charred furniture tumbled in the ruined garden amid broken glass. Up, up, up rattled the train to the top of a ledge with a view down a ravine where a wrecked car had been abandoned to the weeds, its blue paint faded, rust lines scribing a map to nowhere scratched into its crumpled metal. A bumper sticker partly scraped off its back wanted to know: DO YO LLOW JESUS THI LOSE?

'I spy: something blue,' I said.

'That's easy!' said Mother. 'It's the shirt that man's wearing, the one standing in the water with that other man.'

'Sure, Mother,' I said, 'you got me. That's it, all right. That's exactly what I was looking at.' Along the bank of a stream flowing at the ravine's bottom were a couple of prospectors panning for gold in the shallow waters, one of them, sure enough, in a blue plaid shirt.

'What are they doing?' Mother asked.

'Looking for gold, I suppose.'

'How do we know if they're finding anything?'

'I guess we can come back in a month and see if they have younger wives and new cars,' I said.

'I can see shiny bits in their basket thingies,' Mother said. 'Is that gold?'

I squinted and thought I could maybe see shimmering glints amid the silt.

'Could be,' I said.

My phone trembled. 'Hang on,' I told Mother, 'Let me see who this is.' It went to voicemail just as I pulled the phone out of my pocket.

'Hello, this is a message for Karen Copperidge from the Human Resources Department of Welco Pharmaceuticals. We recently received your resumé and application for a job in Customer Service and would like to schedule an interview with you as soon as possible. Please call us back at this number at your earliest convenience.'

'I'm going upstairs to call them back – reception is probably spotty down here,' I said.

'That's not fair! It was my turn to be Spy!'

'I'll be right back, Mother – this is important.'

It had become dark and I turned on the kitchen light. For a second I thought I smelled gas, but decided I was imagining it. I called the number back and got a recording: 'Para español, oprima el numero dos.' I waited for the English message, but it never came. I hung up and called back, thinking I'd caught the message mid-loop. The same thing happened four more times, and I finally pressed 2.

Another recording. 'Sentimos que no haya nadie para atender su llamada. Por favor intente volver a llamar durante el horario comercial y ¡tenga un buen día!'

Crap.

I kept the phone to my ear for a moment as if a live, English-speaking person could be willed to come on the line. I turned on the tap to pour myself a glass of water but nothing happened. The lights flickered and went out and I drew back the curtain from the kitchen window to see if anyone else's lights were on. Pitch black. Not a single light, not even from traffic. My phone's flashlight revealed earth pressed against glass. I backed away and went to the door, opened it and stepped aside as a small landslide tumbled over the linoleum. Part of a yellow ribcage from some long-interred animal disgorged itself from the shifting earth. I was too stunned to panic. At the top of the basement stairs, I hollered, 'Mother?'

'We're down here!' Mother said.

I followed the light from my phone's flashlight down the stairs. 'The house got buried!'

'Sinkhole,' a deep voice said.

'Who's that?' I asked.

'That's Baby,' Mother said.

'Baby?'

'Sure; Baby. Mothers have babies and I have Baby.' Mother blew out a match she had used to light some candles. 'I was afraid you weren't coming back, so I made Baby come keep me company.'

Baby sat in a musty recliner, stubbled face partly in shadow, his t-shirt glowing in the light of the cigar scissored in his hairy fingers. He smelled like lost change excavated from the trapped gunk between cushions.

'He better not be expecting me to feed him,' I said.

'I'm good,' Baby said, 'Found the beer.'

'He's my smart boy,' said Mother, patting him on the arm.

'I hope you're not a loud swallower,' I said.

Baby belched. Like Mother, like son. I turned to her.

'Jesus, Mother, I only went up to make one quick phone call.'

Mother and Baby exchanged a look.

'What should we do about the sinkhole?' I asked. 'Should we call somebody? Should we see if we can get to the roof? What's the protocol?'

'Been happening all over this part of town. Places sitting pretty one minute, gone the next. Swallowed whole,' Baby said. 'Who knows how deep we're in? Relax, lady. I'm sure the authorities are taking care of everything. All we citizens can do is sit tight.'

'Happening all over? This is the first I've heard of it,' I said.

'See what I mean?' Mother said to Baby, 'Too depressed or something to notice what's going on. This is what I've been putting up with.' She threw her little arms up and turned back to the train set. The engine was stuck halfway out of a tunnel.

'I definitely think I saw them getting gold,' said Mother. 'I'm going to pretend I'm tiny and go have a look.'

Baby ejected himself from the chair, hitched up his pants, and toddled over to the train table. 'Just look at that mini-Anytown set smack in the middle of America the Beeyoutiful, will you?' said Baby. 'I think I'll come with you.'

'Good Baby!' said Mother, 'Clever Baby! I can't leave you by yourself, and I sure don't trust that one.' She pointed her chin in my direction.

'You're leaving me?' I said.

'Come if you want to,' said Mother. 'I don't care.'

'Yeah,' Baby said, 'we don't care.'

I punched him in the face. Blood turtled out of one nostril.

'Shut up, Baby,' I said.

'Ow.' He touched the blood and held his fingers out to look, 'That hurt.'

'*Uh*-oh – *some*body's *jeal*ous,' sang Mother.

'Maybe I'll catch up with you later,' I said. 'I'm going to try to get someone on the phone, see if there's daylight somewhere. Maybe the crawlspace in the attic. I'm not convinced anyone's trying to dig us out.'

'Suit yourself,' said Mother. 'But don't forget: finders keepers!' She looked down at her sneakers. One of them was untied and she held her foot up to me. I double-knotted the bow and wiped her nose with a used tissue. 'Off you go, then,' I said. 'Good luck.'

As soon as she was gone, I missed Mother. If I ever got out of here, I could imagine myself telling stories about her – and Baby, too, though no one would believe me. The warm spot he'd left in the chair was unsettling, but I sat there and finished his beer. I could hear the liquid squirming through my bowels. My phone whimpered briefly against my skin but I ignored it. I watched the two of them walk through the graveyard, past the mourners, and toward the stream. The prospectors looked like they hadn't moved much although the guy in the blue plaid shirt had rolled his sleeves up past his elbows since I'd last looked. When

Baby got to the panty-covered headstone, he put his hand on the crotch and I thought I heard him snicker. Mother kicked a plastic aster at the stone's base. They walked until they were trampling the bracken at water's edge. Neither of them looked back.

Chris Kohler

Pipe

They'll tell you that just about anything is good for you, but I'll tell you what's not good for you is crawling inside a pipe. Not good in any way they would understand it, because it's not a nook or a cubby hole, it has no warmth, it's a circle which keeps going, and its bottom is sometimes full of water and sometimes not.

I don't really know why I crawled inside it, but I know that I will never regret it and that I will go to my grave with dignity and ignorance. Ignorance at the world that has passed me by outside the pipe. And dignity, held inside my heart, in pride of my actions and my attempt at individuality.

If I had known that after crawling too far into the pipe to crawl back, I would find someone else there, I would have either found a different pipe to crawl into, or maybe just tried to think of something else to do, which would also express my pride and dignity. But my life has been lived as a dog that lies down, rolls over and gives the paw in expectation of a treat which was given once and never given again. So that after the idea of crawling into a pipe edged its way from blind spots between my eyes and into full vision, after I made plans of a kind, then found a pipe and crawled into it, and then encountered a pair of fidgeting shoes, another person inside the pipe, I thought, this is typical.

God knows what she was doing in the pipe. I never asked. Mostly because I thought, what if she asks me and I have to give an answer before I am really ready. Because mostly the reason I had for crawling inside was to find out why I had thought of it in the first place, and why I often found myself thinking of nothing else.

I stared in anger at her shoes, not knowing if she knew I was there. Until I tried to take space. I pushed my head against her feet, but all she did was bunch up her knees, then push some of the dirt and water at the bottom of the pipe into my mouth and face, so that I had to retreat.

Then she tried to take space, and she forced me back a long distance by that method. Until I found that her knees were tickly and she flinched and muted some laughter, then scraped her way away from me.

My first plan had been to get to the other side of the pipe and then think about the possibilities of leaving and thinking over what I had done. But what with her being inside it, I began to give up on that idea and see that staying put and living in the pipe was better and more complete and just the kind of thing that they wouldn't be able to say was good for you.

In the years that I lived before my idea, I had grown very sick of what was good. They said that closing your eyes was good, that opening them was good, that breathing and speaking was good and that the movements of your body were good. Even though we can see every day that our nails, our hair, our food and our water are desperate to escape us. I wanted to do what was not good, so I crawled inside the pipe.

At first being there was just like pulling on a jumper and not finding the neck hole, having to go on and on in wool and linen. Lost. Stepping inside the jumper and wondering, am I in the arm? Am I in the belly? The breast? The waistband or worse, between the purls. The pipe went on forever with no twinkling glint at the end. But anyone who has been in a room they don't know or can't trust or struggle to see in, will know that there is always a two second escape from other people inside the jumper. Closing your eyes in there, that's a real pleasure.

I wouldn't have said I was a nervous man until I felt the trembling stop. It was as if the note which the world played had changed, a low hum and tremor had shifted pitch. A permanent earthquake ended. And the air was clear and open and I felt its space. The rounded pipe was a very comfortable cavern that I shouted into and encountered myself, my echo. And then I met her that I have called Mary.

I called her that, because I approached her feet and held them like they were the foot of the cross, and there I was becoming Magdalene or the mother of Jesus. So being sensible I should have called myself Mary and not been embarrassed of it, but even two people in a pipe, that's a society and no matter how you break out of the world what are you? You're the graft of one tree put into the trunk of another and all you try to do is bloom your own old colour while every branch around you is all the same, bright white. To tell a personal story, my Grandfather had a cherry tree in which he grafted a pink branch. It's only what comes to mind. Over time we saw that the new blooms faded and bleached into white. So I switched it around and I called her Mary, because although I asked her name, and although she answered, the pipe stifled the words that came back to me. I never heard them clearly, or the words that she said were impossible, unconnected words. It wasn't idyllic, but then it couldn't have been.

What the man poured on us I don't know. We had moved close to the uppermost part of the pipe, in order to hear what went on at that side of the hill. We saw legs moving and boots, then the edge of a bucket and then what he poured down over us. It ran shallow down the pipe, under our mouths and over our chests and legs. Its surface swirled with colour like petrol but it didn't smell like it. It was sharp in my mouth, and in my lungs it began to ache. He threw it right down the pipe and it must have gotten to her first. Why he did it I don't know. Because we were in the pipe and obstructing it? Or because he thought the pipe was empty and led to a sewer? I don't know. I never heard her cough or splutter, but she reacted when I did. She flinched in fright as if she was waking up afraid, confusing me with what had been in her dream. As I coughed she kicked back at my hands and face, so I crawled back away from her. Was the man trying to dissolve us? Clear us away? Have us broken down to slops? The pain in my eyes, the taste in my mouth. I needed to breath, did she not too? Or did she wait, then move forward to her own side of the hill instead of mine? I pushed myself back, given that she would not go forward. What he poured was shallow all through the pipe, in front of my mouth, soaking into my clothes. When I finally felt rain on my legs, on my chest, and then on my face, I could see why they would want what was good. I could see why the world was for us. I could see how hard it was to make one for yourself.

Coughing, I walked back along the streets where I had once been upright. My legs began to break themselves in, with long strides the length of me! All my height and these vast shoulders, the air on my face, the warmth of sunlight, the contradiction of the cold in the wind, I enjoyed it. I returned to the house I had, who knows if it was mine now. The back door was lying half open and I walked into the kitchen. I struggled to remember what the wallpaper had been or what the table and chairs had been like, who knows, who can think of these things.

I ran the tap and felt the liquid that the man had thrown separating over my skin. It pulled tight at the corners of my eyes, stinging there and pulling further. Into my mouth. A tooth felt loose. I turned myself about under the tap and near drowned. I pulled open the cupboards below the sink, looking for a cloth or some product that could strip me of what had been poured. What I saw instead, below the sink, behind the u bend which flexed and cracked as I looked in, was a pair of feet fidgeting, then disappearing to follow a pair of legs and arms and a head which must have been in the wall. I stood back in fright. If they hadn't been so different, I would have imagined that these were Mary's feet. But I have never been lucky. A joyful ghost never haunts a man, and a shadow is dark, and only disappears when the world is dark. That's all my worldly wisdom.

I heard the noise of the man in the wall and I went for the drawer where I had kept the knives. It was full of tea towels and table runners, embroidered with flowers and abstracted shapes, and there below the first table cloth, an elbow turned itself away, then flinched and disappeared back into the wall I suppose. Not the first man, but another. I kicked the drawer shut. Is this what they're saying is good now? Or is it what people might do against that? I don't know. I kicked the drawer again. My body was all creepy crawlies just thinking about the noises I was hearing.

I dragged back the washing machine and saw there another pair of feet. Not hers, I've never been lucky. Under the sink, another pair. In the chimney that I don't remember ever lighting, the fingertips of a man hanging upside down. It will drive me half mad to think about them. They don't speak, it must be the style. But I don't know if it is something that they were told while I was in the pipe, which might invalidate the pipe and surely, set her free of it? Or it might be something they have taken to themselves? Crawling. Holding. Staying put. I don't know.

I heard a key in the lock. Like a scuttling rat I pelted upstairs and found a space where there was only the shins of a man, with his head buried down into his knees and his arms tight around them. I stuck my elbow right in and climbed over and kicked him twice. I remember once how I trained a dog. I stuck their muzzle in it. So I pushed his head down, then pushed away from him. It was the cupboard and I was sitting on their shoes. My head was in trouser legs and dresses. In pockets, in coat hangers. The man retreated, they have made holes everywhere they can fit through. I heard the footsteps come close and then the cupboard opened.

I was welcomed back. The house was still mine although my family had moved in. I was given a room of it. Granddad Granddad Granddad, the youngest call me. I lived a whole life in spaces smaller than your bed, I always say. Dad Dad Dad, one calls me. Tell me about your life before us, he says, and keeps me in this room. How do you live in terror and in peace among people? Not to know anymore what is good. To live in the walls or in the rooms. Or maybe to find Mary and marry her. If they call me Granddad, then life is marching on. 'Make a decision!' I want to shout. If only I knew what was good.

At night, in darkness so deep that I could mistake my bed for the rounded concrete of the pipe, I sometimes say to myself, 'It takes a lot of strength to have left the pipe,' and it comforts me. But if I am honest, I know that it takes a lot more strength to have stayed put and I admire her. Even when it is madness, even if you have forgotten the reasons, even if what was thrown is still there, even if you kick your legs back and there is no one still there to push you back.

I wish that what I had done was found her, then crawled back out the pipe and walked right round the hill and crawled in the other way to see her face, though I suspect that I would only find that she had crawled in hands first and couldn't see me, though she could hold my face in her hands which would be a comfort.

I thought about getting a kilt and a minister and setting them up at one end and lighting a fire at the other but you have to be sensible about these things, and patient and slow.

So sometimes I walk out to the hill and shout into the pipe and maybe she can hear me or maybe she crawled out a long time ago and never came to find me or couldn't find me or got herself lost, but anyway I just keep shouting or sometimes just talking as if she had crawled backwards and was lying right up close in the shadows where I couldn't see her.

I say, 'Please Mary, why don't you come outside? Out here there's so many ways to have been treated. I've been kicked and stepped over and laid down next to and held. I've been grabbed by the shoulders and the waist and by an ankle and a wrist I've pulled down to the floor, to a bed and once into a car. I've been followed and doused and poked in the eye. And I've been kissed and whispered over and tied in a bundle. Someone's always sitting on my knee and someone else is always jumping over me. There's a person in every crook of this house. Why isn't one of them you, Mary, why not come outside?'

Maybe she can hear me when I'm talking or maybe she can't or maybe again there's someone else in there by now who might pass on the message or just take what I'm saying to heart themselves. I don't believe that there's ever a word spoken which is wasted, they all fall down like leaves at the base of a tree and even though they rot they end up broken down and back inside the tree again soon enough and even though you had a bad idea there might be a new way to express it even if it is just to say that crawling inside a pipe isn't worth the hassle, don't pretend to me that it is.

Nicolette Polek

Two Fictions

DOORSTOP

My mother has a two-pound doorstop that she uses in the summer. It's a souvenir copy of the original kilogram. She got it on a tour of the Department of Measurements in Sevres, France, where the original kilogram is kept in a triple-locked vault in the basement.

Three people have the key to the vault, so they can polish it by hand, and compare it to other sister copies, which they do every few years. In 2009, the block was shrinking. In 2013, growing. This, in Sevres, of all places. A city where people are notoriously and comically, according to my mother, unable to adapt to change.

In seventh grade, my best friend moved away to go to a special math high school. I spent the ensuing week despairing, and my mother threatened to send me to that little French city, where the people were so anxious for the kilogram block, she said, that they sat forever in tears, frigid and stupid. Maybe then I'd learn.

I am in my thirties now, living at home again. My brother is dying, and I broke up with my boyfriend. My mother is afraid to answer the phone when it rings, has always been, so I answer. But first, I prop open the door, let the wind in.

A girl is pushing an old man down the hallway, and they pass many windows out of which the old man cannot see.

The place she's taking him, she says, is bright and at a perfect temperature and humidity level. There will be towels and a toothbrush and a bowl of candied dates that he especially likes. There are newly added massage chairs and a cabinet filled with handwarmers, markers, and AA batteries, and when he gets there, he can write whatever he likes on his nametag.

A woman approaches them and hands the old man a clipboard with forms to fill out regarding the place. She chimes in, saying that the place 'is entirely covered in a blue-ish light,' that there are trees to sit under if he wants to be alone, and small animals that will protect him. There is a black porcelain swimming pool filled with many beautiful people who are excited to meet him, and he will be given elegant grey stockings to wear.

Where he is being taken, wires are obsolete, and at night there is a hidden table for him to eat cookies and gaze up at the moon. The man gives the woman back the clipboard, and she blows him a kiss before disappearing behind a door that they pass.

The girl and the old man stop in a small restaurant and split a strawberry pie. 'We're almost there,' she says, and the waitress tells the old man that he will be able to see the whole place at once, and in the distance, he will see a house from which his mother looks out at him fondly.

After they finish eating, the girl pushes faster down the hallways, turning left and right, so the windows pass quickly when the old man stretches his neck towards them. She tells him that he deserves to live in this place, and that this is the place just for him.

The hallways slowly start to dim, from the days-worth of travel. The trip to where the old man is being taken is a bit long, so the girl pauses to use the restroom, leaving him behind. Many people are walking down the hallway, in a hurry to get to their homes, and must move around the old man, causing them to occasionally bump into each other.

One person drops her coffee and file folder. As she picks up her things, the old man tells her where he is going, to which she says 'I know a few people there, and they are all very happy.' She has a dog with her, who makes a cheerful sound when hearing about the place. The old man wants to pet the dog's head, but the person is in a hurry and leaves.

A couple, who the old man does not recognize, moves the old man to the side of the hallway, puts him in an elevator, then wheels him into a small room. When he tries to tell them where he is going, they furrow their brows and tell the old man that the place does not exist. They turn off the light and close the door, so the people no longer have to walk around him.

The room is empty and clean. There is a crack from under the door, which is how the light gets in.

He waits there, and folds his hands in his lap.

He waits there, imagining the things that the girl told him, about the tropical trees.

He thinks about the many seagulls to count as he goes to sleep. Almost a hundred seagulls, she had said.

Babak Lakghomi

Everything Green

They have shaved half of Mother's hair and her voice sounds like a pump trying to prime itself.

In that voice, she instructs me to boil the water and add rice to the boiling pot. She asks me to help her in the shower.

She sits on a plastic bucket. I rub the washcloth on her back. I open her fingers to clean the space between, like her hands used to do mine. Mother's hands are soft hands, small hands, not like mine – mine are like my father's, fingers long and knuckles fat.

I fill up a small tub and pour water on her head. Then, Mother asks me to leave. From the other side of the door, I hear her struggle to take off her bra, her panties – the bucket and the stick her only aids. She comes out of the shower, her face flushed, a white towel wrapped around her waist. Sweat drips from her forehead.

My father is in another town working for a garlic powder factory. When he comes back, I can smell garlic and alcohol. Thank God Mother can't smell anymore.

Mother says she sees everything green. The sun is bleeding in this green landscape.

An ambulance takes her back to the hospital.

I stay in the house. I eat food frosted in the fridge, food foil-wrapped by neighbours. Fluorescent lamps hum in the empty house.

At night, I leave the TV on. A woman dances naked covering her nipples with rose petals. In a public bath, a girl takes a boy into his mouth.

I open Mother's dresser, my fingers stroking the silk of her panties.

When Mother returns, this is not Mother – her soft hands that sift the rice, spreading my socks on the heater. Her bottle of perfume collects dust on the dresser.

I lie down by her side on her bed trying to smell the smell that was hers.

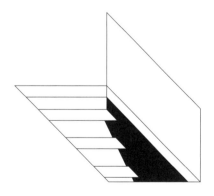

Natalie Ferris

A Wrench is Known as an English Key

Language is a labyrinth of paths
— LUDWIG WITTGENSTEIN

The first time I saw the films of Ana Hatherly, the rain was waiting in the clouds. Tigre de Papel, a small bookshop in the Arroios district of Lisbon, was hosting a small evening celebration of her work. Brown plastic chairs had been arranged in a circle and placed at the back of the room. I chose the seat that would obscure me the most, nervous of my elementary grasp of both the language and the evening's subject, and tucked myself away beside a large bookcase. It smelt new. Every surface, from floor to wall to ceiling, was seamlessly overlaid with chipboard, as if one of the back rooms in which these films were originally viewed had been cast. The focal point was a thin, translucent sheet pinned up over one of the central bookcases, flickering as the wind outside began to pick up. Through the fabric the spines of books left their impression in the light of the projector, a detail I felt Hatherly would have enjoyed. The room had filled, seats occupied by bodies slick with the sudden rain. A few words were said to introduce her *curtas-metragens* before her enigmatic ciphers began to dance across the screen. I had come because, even in my limited exposure to her work and brittle knowledge of the language in which she worked, I felt so deeply connected to her puzzling vision of life, language, action, and creativity. A friend had shown me two small reproductions of drawings from Hatherly's *a reinvenção de leitura* (1975), visual fields of intricately written script, and I was riveted by the trailing lines that looped like troubled thoughts and snagged at the end of her pen. In those early months of living in Lisbon, Portuguese was a language that still held me at arm's length, and yet in her I found kinship with a darting, unsettled view of letters, words and their meanings. She gave me license to inhabit the strangeness.

The films on show that evening were the product of a landmark moment in the history of modern Portugal. Hatherly was in London for the early months of 1974, having spent three years studying film and animation at the London Film School. En route to Egypt in April of that year, presumably to spend time with the designs, figures, and glyphs that had come to loom so large in her calligraphic work, she decided to make a brief stop in Portugal. She made her opportune arrival in Lisbon on 25 April 1974, the day of the Carnation Revolution. Some years later Hatherly recalled the augur of that dawn flight from London, ablaze with colour, drinking orange juice while watching the sunrise through the window, a 'transparent bloody egg'. She never completed her journey, remaining in the city to witness 'this moment of exaltation', 'of great euphoria, great freedom and great enthusiasm', taking to the streets and recording what she saw while staying with friends such as the artists Ernesto de Sousa and Mário Cesariny. Filmed with a Super 8 camera, the film '*Revolução*' (1975) is a roving eye on the streets of Lisbon that focuses on the ephemeral traces of popular protest.[1] Her camera pitches at a pace over the political posters, graffiti, revolutionary murals, pamphlets, and newspaper photographs encountered on the streets and in the press, capturing the feverish energy of that decisive period. It is a collagistic film, and with a strobe-like effect her lens judders over slogans, images, and communist iconography, much of which had been hand-painted, to the brisk tempo of chanting crowds, protest speeches, and revolutionary songs, such as Zeca Afonso's pivotal 'Grândola, Vila Morena'. Animated by the flickering of the focus, the images appear to move as if bobbing above a crowd, thrust into the sky by the hands of demonstrators or viewed while marching past. A fiery sun of yellow and orange chalk bears the word 'Liberdade' ('freedom') in an arc at its centre, heralding this new dawn for Portugal.

Over the course of a single day the coup, engineered by several hundred lieutenants, captains and majors under the *Movimento das Forças Armadas* (MFA), managed to topple the authoritarian regime of the Estado Novo, which had held the country in its grip for almost half a century. Under the rule of two Prime Ministers, António de Oliveira Salazar from 1932 to 1968, and Marcelo Caetano from 1968 until 1974, Portugal had endured decades of totalitarian control,

---

1 Ana Hatherly, '*Revolução*' (1975), 11 min.

economic injustice, social repression and colonial wars fought on many fronts, leaving the military and the people eager for change. It was famously a near blood-less revolution, in spite of the swathes of red of every shade – ruby, carmine, rust – that frequently colour Hatherly's film. Aside from its associations with com-munism, the prevailing political temper of the revo-lution, red also became a symbol of freedom, origi-nating in the simple act of Celeste Caeiro, a restaurant worker who distributed the many red carnations her restaurant had bought to hand to new customers. She offered flowers to the soldiers headed for Largo do Carmo, a gesture that spread to other flower-sellers in the city centre. The soldiers loaded bunches of red carnations into the barrels of their tanks, inserted them into the muzzles of their rifles, pinned them to their uniforms, while Lisboetas tucked them behind their ears or brandished them in their hands. It's one of the most striking aspects of the photographs that remain from that day – scarlet blooms springing from every-where, twined around brooches, flags, car aerials, bal-conies – and in those following, the carnation blown up to occupy banners the scale of buildings.

The flower did not loom so large in Hatherly's imagination. Few appear in her films, collages or drawings of this period. For her, it was the language of revolution – written onto walls, typed up on notic-es, daubed onto monuments – that had to live beyond the spectacle of that day. These words were evidence, scraps of testimony to be preserved and reclaimed, particularly as uncertainty reigned over the ensuing eighteen months and held little of the promise of those late April days. The ferocity of phrases such as 'Poesia ou Morte' ('Poetry or Death'), daubed onto the back of road traffic signs along the Marginal, had been flayed by the salt in the air. The revolution 'blew [her] away', along with her familial roots in Lisbon. Hatherly had to sell her home, her furniture and many of her possessions, entering a period of great financial difficulty. What had the revolution come to mean? What relevance did the word 'revolution' continue to hold? What shape, if any, could it now take? Hatherly designed several ink drawings and acrylic paintings that probed the dissolution of meaning faced with growing socio-political confusion. '*Desenho* (*Revolução*)' (1975) depicts two central forms composed entirely of stacked handwritten script, a capital 'I' and a lambda. They could be architectural structures, a tower and an arch built entirely from single repetitions of the noun, '*a revolução*'. The script routinely loses its regularity, loosening writing's pact with legibility, and clusters into tight chaotic black clouds of scrawls that spiral off into fine lines of unreadable script. It is as if the pillars, along with words, are dissolving into the atmosphere. Language never quite fails her, however; the pillars remain standing and shapes of letters are faintly apparent in the coiling of her marks. Although she makes the legible illegible, language is still supremely visible.

The writing in her work swiftly became the writing of others. Entertaining chance encounters with her materials, she walked the streets in the months that followed the revolution and stripped the urban landscape of its faded, fragmented, exclamatory handwriting, typography, and imagery, for use in the series *As Ruas de Lisboa* (1977). She tore, crumpled, and reassembled her collated items into collages that faithfully represented their native disorder. Red is the prevailing colour, torn from advertisements for the travelling circus, rally posters of the Partido Socialista or reproductions of the *Bandeira das Quinas*. It was 'a way of fixing', she noted later, 'through a certain form of mural writing, an entire period in the life of the city and the life of the country that is already beginning to look remote'. She was returning the city to its reinventors. However, much like her ink drawings, the collages do not celebrate revolutionary chaos, but in their heightened, textured surfaces inveigh against the flatlining of popular energies. One features a bold line of repeated question marks, an absurdist gesture that agitates the viewer into asking questions of their own relationship to collective uncertainty. Hatherly frequently turned to the verb *arrancar*, 'to wrench', when describing her attitude towards language and writing in the wake of revolution. She felt a responsibility to 'wrench' words free of their fastenings, to emancipate them from the petrified façade of established discourse, and to craft new alliances between world and word. Her work of the 1960s had been constructive, creating a basis for concrete and experimental poetry in Portugal as part of the PO-EX movement, along-

side poets such as António Aragão and E. M. de Melo
e Castro. Her new abecedaries 'Ideograma Estrutural'
(1966) and 'Alfabeto Estrutural' (1967) and her asemic
drawings of the late 1960s devised a strong ideologi-
cal framework whereby the hand, schooled in many
archaic writing systems, sought to communicate the
gestural foundations of language. Now, in books such
as *a reinvenção de leitura* (1975) and *o escritor* (1975), and
radical performances such as *'poema d'entro'* (1976) and
'rotura' (1977), her writing spun into dark vortices, her
hand slashed through sheets of suspended paper, and
pasted letters cascaded from open mouths. What hap-
pens when the relationship to both world and word
begins to buckle?

. . .

The alchemical symbol for water is a downward
pointing triangle. Upended, one point plunges towards the unknown. The rain in Lisbon often made
me think of notation. I know this sounds too romantic,
too neat, particularly for a rain that would often fall in
unruly sheets, dislodging cobbles, stripping trees, and
running thick with dirt and small brown beer bottles.
But there was something in the geometry of its fall,
these rods driven by wind that would swing and drive
in an arc of directions, backlit by the amber lamplight,
crossing with the diagonal lines of the tall buildings
opposite. Each long strip of water was visible, and, in
the laboured rate of its fall, traceable. They were marks

made along a stave, playing havoc with the tension of washing lines, iron fretwork, squared tiling. Perhaps I had begun to see strikethroughs everywhere, head full of living my days in a new language, slight grey lines lifting from the pages of exercise books to fall around me with every repeated mistake. 'All is the rain's, [...] And all we hear and feel and know and see/Is wrapt around as with a masking cloak', wrote Fernando Pessoa, in one of several poems about the 'slanting', 'silencing', 'whispering' powers of the rain in Lisbon. Rain, for Pessoa, had the ability to numb or over-whelm, but also the potential to recolour the world, impart mysteries, speak truths to the soul. There was an exclamatory force to this Atlantic rain, in its sud-den hot bursts quite unlike the bleary drizzle of home. Sometimes it was warm, as if swilled in the mouth. Portuguese is a language full of the rush of its weather. *Chuva*, the word for rain, or *chuvoso*, rainy, summons the lips into an evocative hush, coercing the voice into an understanding with the veils of water outside. In those days I lived a life largely seized from the lips of others, phrases heard in the quiosques, inferred from telenovelas, seen on packaging, caught across a dinner table, gleaned from newstands. I parroted what I heard or channeled my needs, desires, opinions through oth-ers, while I made the slow progress towards inventing for myself. On our third meeting, Isabel, the young writer who taught me Portuguese, pressed her book of short stories into my hands, entitled, *Não Te Es-queças Do Guarda-Chuva* ('Do Not Forget Your Umbrella'). It felt like a call to arms, a motion to head out into the rain.

Concrete poetry found one of its forebears in a poem about rain, 'Il Pleut', by Guillaume Apollinaire, an avant-garde manifestation 'Calligramme' of what in Latin poetry is known as *carmen figuratum* (figured poems). It is tempting to see water in Hatherly's 'drawing-writings', and to read her flowing lines as tidal surges overturning the rectilinearity of typeset texts. In drawings such as 'Salva a Alma!' ('Save the Soul!'), the cover image for her book *A Idade da Escrita* (1998), lines of script billow and trail to create a form of jellyfish-like buoyancy. Others from the same collection are similarly formed of twisting lines of words, flowing currents that converge and spill away, spun into frothy masses, fragments or letters flying like spray into the spine of the book. Several, in their irregular crosshatching, appear like frayed nets raised from the seabed. There is a quality of something shifting, something poured, in these pages, a stream of consciousness method made evident when observing videos of Hatherly drawing or etching. With close attention to her prepared surface, small squares measured onto paper or cut from copper plates, her hand moves rapidly, instinctively, and continuously, rarely breaking the pen's contact with the surface so that a single line may span the entire duration of the drawing. Shortly after the revolution, Hatherly pledged to 'live intensely each moment as it occurs' and to channel this impulsiveness into her work. She sought an immediacy of representation through changes in writerly register, employing cursive script, composing on her scattering the page with letraset, or, towards the end of her life, using spray paint. There is a glimmer of her purpose in André Breton's 1924 definition of surrealism as 'psychic automatism [...] by which one proposes to express – verbally, by means of the written word, or in any other manner – the actual functioning of thought'. Visual parallels can be drawn between the apparent free-flow of Hatherly's ink drawings of the 1980s and 1990s and the automatic drawings of André Masson and Jean Arp, the arrows in certain of Paul Klee's abstract grids, or the mescaline drawings of Henri Michaux. However, her works on paper or in space are not guided purely by the meanderings of the subconscious, as esoteric projections of dreams, imaginings, trances or meditative thinking, or with any of the ease of liquid flow, but by a body steeped in the history of chirography.

Hatherly's practice was guided by the gestures of the *mão inteligente* (the intelligent hand). The hand could be trained to reproduce fathomless communicative forms – across regions, across cultures, across time – and in its learning come to acquire for itself 'the knowledge of the creative act and the gratuitous gesture'. As a scholar of ancient, classical, early modern and modern writing systems, and particularly of the art and literature of the Baroque period, Hatherly assumed the gestures of countless scribes before her. 'The basis of all my work is still and always the same,'

she asserted on film in 2002, 'It is an exploration of
the concepts of writing'. Vitally, this education was
not always couched in languages that were comprehensible to her, but often 'non-readable' characters
or marks. She understood both the gestural genesis
of all language and the intuition that thought exists
as raw matter to be disfigured by language. Beginning with the close scrutiny of ancient Chinese in the
1960s, she, as discussed in correspondence with Dom
Sylvester Houédard, also prioritised the 'prior cen-
turies of experiments with image-texts, comprised
of hieroglyphs, ideograms, cryptograms, diagrams,
rebuses, mandalas, amulets, jewels, toys, gravestones,
and even some monuments, besides all other poematic
texts or objects'.[2] Engaging only her unschooled eye
to perceive their mysterious resemblances and shared
etymologies, Hatherly's aim was to 'extend the field
of reading beyond literality', but also to 'widen the
field of formal research' and 'enlarge the creative field
for writing itself'. Beyond formal experimentation,
it was an interest cultivated amidst twentieth-centu-
ry investigations into the problems of representation
and communication. Her essays and poetry teem with
voices drawn from philosophy, structuralism, material culture, modernism, anthropology: Roland

2 Ana Hatherly, 'Short Essay', in *PO.EX: Essays from Portugal on
Cyberliterature and Intermedia*, ed. by Sandy Baldwin and Rui Tor-
res (Morgantown, WV: Center for Literary Computing, 2014),
pp. 49–64, pp. 49–50.

Barthes, Max Bense, Ernst Cassirer, E. H. Gombrich, Johan Huizinga, James Joyce, Julia Kristeva, Stéphane Mallarmé, Claude Levi-Strauss, Ludwig Wittgenstein. The intelligent hand would open the 'closed loop of language', in its willingness to play with new means of signification, and create a new universal language based upon the recognition of the essential ambiguity of all language.[3]

My mind would often run to her silhouettes of searching hands when failing to find my words in Portuguese, wringing mine in exasperation. Hands, as opaque forms or outlines poised with a pen, are recurrent subjects in Hatherly's work, appearing in a range of illusory ways that betray the hand of the artist. Hatherly spent her early years training as a pianist, studying at the Lisbon Conservatoire, which perhaps gave her a feeling for the dexterity and ingenuity to be achieved by the fingertips. Unlike the motif observed in many medieval and renaissance manuscripts, in which manicules (small hands drawn by scribes) would beckon or point from margins to particular words or passages in a text, Hatherly's hands are seen busy in the act of crafting her 'drawing-writings': a hand appears to paint typewritten letters, a steady hand loses its concentration, another holds in wait before a blank page. She thought of herself as 'an artificer', who 'manipulates and questions the materials' with which she worked, and the presence of these hands remind the

---

3 Mapas.

viewer of the technical trickery employed by every writer or artist. Hatherly's deep affinity for the art and literature of the Baroque period was primarily founded upon its celebration of artifice, performance, illusion, and play.[4] She found in the Baroque what some of her avant-garde contemporaries had also begun to discover: models for the kinds of conceptual experiment that would disrupt the artistic ideals established by the authoritarian regime, such as purity, unity, authority, and certainty. She wanted to push literature beyond this immobility, break it down, remould it, and revel in the creative act as a game that worked in tandem with inventive approaches to form, like the puzzles, puns, myths, mirrors, maps, riddles, clues, acrostics, and labyrinths of the Baroque imagination.

For Hatherly, the acknowledgement of these works was tantamount to a political act, exalting the practice of play to upset the status quo. She invented an abstract deck of cards for the writer, presumably to be shuffled, dealt, and handled; a scroll that unfurls to reveal a cryptic message thronged with shadows; and a box of plastic letters twined together to form an alternative alphabet.[5] Projects such as *Anagramas* (1969), *Anagramático* (1970), and *Isto É Uma Experência (O Computador Sem Mestre)* (n.d.) [This is an Experience (The Computer Without Master)] and drawings such as *Puzzle Carta de Amor* (1998) and *Labirinto Urbano*

---

4 Gulbenkian exhibition.
5 *O Jogo do Escritor I & II* (1970) [*The Game of the Writer I & II*].

(1999) all take inspiration from Baroque forms of encipherment and visual contortion. They are works to be solved, comic propositions that ask a reader to follow their workings and determine their process. Her words and phrases in these projects fold back on themselves, enter dizzying coils, reach dead ends, reflect one another, multiply and remake themselves into manifold versions. She makes and remakes these riddles to discover a new mode of narrative, one buried beneath those uses and experiences of language that have fallen from favour or are not yet known. This orbital play found its high point in a game pursued by Hatherly, Melo e Castro, Aragão and Alberto Pimento, *Joyciana* (1982), a 'homage' to *Finnegans Wake* (1939) by James Joyce in the form of '23 Variations' on lines taken from the novel. Each of these 23 lines collapse into their constituent words and a miscellany of possible words are provided as translations for each word, including both literal and non-literal solutions. Wrenched, as Hatherly would have it, from their context, these words forged new visual and aural connections or equivalences, disarming assumptions to possess and create logics of their own. Language itself can trick and manipulate: *Joyciana* explores the creative potential of the mistake and the promising slips of *falsos cognatos* (false friends) that exist between most languages. The writer was, for Hatherly, a 'calculator of improbabilities', but such literary play was not only an exercise in writerly wit and ingenuity, but also an act intended to empower the reader. A 'wrench' translates as *uma chave inglesa* in Portuguese, 'an English key': it was my 'key' to invention as much as it was Hatherly's, both reader and writer drawn into the effort. In an Oulipian way, Hatherly wrote to explore what literature might be, rather than to say what it is: to look at her work was, for me, a way of observing all the ways in which I do not know. She brought forth, and made her reader bear the burden of, the vast expansiveness of language.

. . .

'Vamos tocar…vamos tocar…vamos tocar', was what I thought I heard. I know now as I knew then that I had heard this command incorrectly, and that it was something far more directive than the phrase as I understood it, 'Let's play'. Meted out at regular intervals almost every Wednesday evening, it signaled a change of pose to the model positioned in the centre of the room. I heard it as an invitation to free the hand, and to be looser, rougher, impulsive. These classes brought me into contact with the body as expressed in Portuguese, with the vocabulary of its movements, gestures, anatomy, expressions, and intimacies. I was learning the language of the body through drawing, trying to assert an image in an environment I often misinterpreted: I drew the wrong side, sketched the wrong detail, produced too quickly or too slowly. Hatherly complained on occasion of the 'exasperating slowness of the hand', but for me it was the mind that was constantly playing catch up. An exercise that re-sembled my hesitancies was the only one of few prob-lems: we would rotate around the model, moving once every minute to occupy chairs placed in an arc, sketching the same pose from different angles to close in on every aspect of the form. It was as if we were twisting a screw ever tighter. In the works of her final years, such as the *Neografitti* series (2001), semi-tex-tual, semi-phallic shapes invaded vast canvases, free-ing her hand in the directional spatter of spray paint. She returned to the physicality of language, crafting anthropomorphic signs, her whole arm engaged in movements now slower and less acute. Drawing for Hatherly was a new language, crafted in the will to see reality as something other than itself. Her guidelines were entirely of her own making.

Sponsors

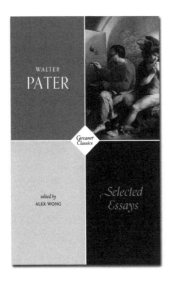
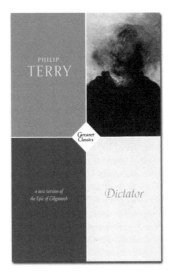

Contributors

Nicole Treska is a writer and professor living in New York City. Her work has appeared in *Epiphany Magazine*, *The Brooklyn Rail*, *The Common* and *Tweed's Magazine of Literature and Art*.

Babak Lakghomi is the author of *Floating Notes* (2018). His fiction has appeared in *NOON*, *New York Tyrant* and *Green Mountains Review* among other places.

Natalie Ferris is a Leverhulme Trust Early Career Fellow in the School of Literatures, Languages & Cultures at the University of Edinburgh. She has contributed to publications such as *Frieze*, *The Guardian*, *The White Review*, *Tate Etc.*, and is currently finalising her monograph *Abstraction in Post-War British Literature* for publication.

Stephen Mortland is a writer living in Indiana.

Cathy Sweeney's short fiction has appeared in *Banshee*, *The Stinging Fly*, *The Dublin Review*, *The Tangerine* and elsewhere.

Rosie Šnajdr's work has appeared as a collection of short stories/episodic novel, *A Hypocritical Reader*, in Isabel Waidner's anthology *Liberating the Canon*, in *#Me Too: A Poetry Collective* published by Chicago Review, and in *Berfrois*. She co-edits *The Cambridge Literary Review*. *We Are Cosmonauts*, a concrete-prose pamphlet, is forthcoming with Hesterglock.

Nicolette Polek is writer and pianist. Her work can be found in *Hotel*, *New York Tyrant Magazine*, *Chicago Quarterly Review*, *Hobart* and elsewhere.

Gordon Lish is traveling until further notice.

Robb Todd is an author, editor and journalist who studied with Gordon Lish. Just one more thing: His cat, a Scottish fold named Columbo, likes to solve mysteries.

Russell Persson lives in Reno, Nevada. His work has appeared in *The Quarterly*, *Unsaid Magazine*, *3:AM Magazine*, *New York Tyrant*, *Fantastic Floridas*, and *Hotel*. His first novel *The Way of Florida* was published in 2017.

Lily Hackett lives in Shepherd's Bush. Her writing has been featured in *New York Tyrant Magazine*, *Egress* and is upcoming in *X-R-A-Y Magazine*.

Catherine Foulkrod is a writer and editor based in Rome, Italy. Her fiction and essays have been published in *New York Tyrant*, *Unsaid*, *Lumina*, *Meridian*, *The Believer*, *Bookforum* and elsewhere.

Kate Wyer lives in Baltimore. Her novel, *Girl, Cow, Monk*, is forthcoming in 2020.

Daryl Scroggins lives in Marfa, Texas. His most recent book is *This Is Not the Way We Came In*.

Wayne Hogan grew up in the Oklahoma hinterlands; failed to finish high school; earned a PhD from Tulane University; served his country in the navy; became a would-be cartoonist.

Gary Lutz's books include *Stories in the Worst Way*, *Divorcer*, *I Looked Alive* and *Partial List of People to Bleach*.

Michael Cuglietta is the author of the forthcoming short fiction collection, *The Feast of Jupiter*. His work has appeared in *NOON*, *The Gettysburg Review*, *Hobart* and elsewhere.

Victoria Lancelotta is the author of *Here in the World: 13 Stories*, and the novels *Far* and *Coeurs Blesses*. She is the recipient of a National Endowment for the Arts Fellowship.

Kathryn Scanlan is the author of *Aug 9–Fog* and *The Dominant Animal* (forthcoming in 2019/2020). Her stories have appeared in *NOON*, *Fence* and Granta. She lives in Los Angeles.

Chris Kohler is a writer living in Glasgow. His work has been published in *Gutter* and *Egress*.

Jason Schwartz is the author of *A German Picturesque* and *John the Posthumous*.

Carrie Cooperider is a writer and visual artist who still doesn't have a website. She lives in New York City, where surely she has access to technology, so what gives?

Brad Phillips is a writer and artist. His *Essays and Fictions* is forthcoming from Tyrant Books.

Julie Reverb is the author of *No Moon*. She is currently working on a novel. Learn more at juliereverb.com

EGRESS welcomes submissions,
including from previously unpublished writers.
No cover letter is necessary.

www.littleislandpress.co.uk/egress